THE WORLD
MORE OR LESS

Jean Rouaud

THE WORLD
MORE OR LESS

*Translated from the French
by Barbara Wright*

ARCADE PUBLISHING
NEW YORK

FIRST NORTH AMERICAN EDITION

First published in France under the title *Le Monde à peu près*

This translation has been published with the financial support of the French Ministry of Culture and Communications.

This is a work of fiction. Names, characters, places, and incidents are either the product of the author's imagination or used fictitiously.

Library of Congress Cataloging-in-Publication Data

Rouaud, Jean,
    [Monde à peu près. English]
    The world more or less / Jean Rouaud ; translated from the French
  by Barbara Wright.
      p. cm.
    ISBN 1-55970-405-5
    I. Wright, Barbara, 1935–   .   II. Title
PQ2678.O7677M6613   1998
843' .914—dc21   97-30001

Published in the United States by Arcade Publishing, Inc., New York
Distributed by Little, Brown and Company

10 9 8 7 6 5 4 3 2 1

BP

PRINTED IN THE UNITED STATES OF AMERICA

THE WORLD
MORE OR LESS

I

I WHO DREAD THE COMPANY of men, whose conversations weary me, it was just my luck, after eight years of strict boarding-school discipline (the only feminine presence being provided by three old nuns with adolescent moustaches), to find myself now among the members of the Logréean Club's reserve team, in the bleak rustic changing room erected alongside what you would have thought was a ploughed field, were it not for its chalk lines and goalposts. And this without any particular inclination on my part, unless, for want of anything better, as a time-honoured cure for Sunday boredom.

But the weather was fit to freeze the tail off a brass monkey. Hence the haste of most of the players, when the final whistle blew, to take refuge within the four jerry-built walls of the shack, everyone making a point of knocking the mud off his boots against the concrete doorstep, thus leaving the ground strewn with cakes of earth punched full of stud holes, before making his way to his place, indicated by the hunchbacked peg his clothes are hanging on, and sitting down more or less wearily, according to his real or suggested state of fatigue, on the communal bench running round the little room that reeks of the combined effluvia of camphorated oil and perspiration. A makeshift shelter: it has rectangular patches of cement between grooved uprights, a green metal door with wired glass which, with the little skylight in the corner over by the showers, allows in the feeble grey light of the winter afternoon, a single-sloping corrugated roof made of some composite material, but this provides sufficient protection against the Atlantic's blend of wind, intense cold and rain, which paralyses the rare spectators now huddling under the awning of the refreshment bar, who make one wonder what pleasure they can possibly derive from such less than fascinating events. But it isn't only boredom, it's also solitude that makes people do strange things. A handful of regulars, from Sunday to Sunday, line up along the guardrail surrounding the pitch (a white tube, with flaking paint, fixed along the top of concrete posts), hunched up, hands in pockets, conspicuously stamping their feet, the bottom of their trousers turned up to protect them from the mud – hence their delicate way of walking on tiptoe – some wearing caps, others with dripping wet hair, but it's odd how in this region, where logically it should be a prerequisite, the raincoat is a rarity, as if its use, or that of an umbrella, would reduce the user to the status of a sissy, a wimp, which would do him no good at all in this all-male society. In any case, most of them are content to turn up the collar of their jacket, the same jacket all year round, the difference between the seasons being merely marked by the addition of a scarf in autumnal colours, even if not knotted, just loosely crossed under the buttoned-up sides of the garment and therefore practically superfluous, thus demonstrating the haughty indifference to the vagaries of the climate shown by those whose wallets have difficulty in adapting to it.

But they are connoisseurs – very much so. You hear them shouting pertinent instructions to the players from the touchline: pass, shoot, clear – easy to say, of course – groaning at a ball lost to an opponent as if at that instant the fate of the world depended on it, momentarily turning their backs as if they can't bear to see any more or have already seen too much. But the world isn't at stake, it's simply a question of manifesting their vexation so as to show the crowd, which consists only of themselves, that they take an interest in the game, or at least that they are trying to convince each other that such is the case. Then why is that boy there keeping the ball to himself when his unmarked teammate has already dived through a breach in the defence and is provoking the first signs of panic in the opposing ranks? It was a heaven-sent opportunity, the ball would already be in the back of the net if that other idiot, me for instance, hadn't gone out of his way to hog the ball and try out unsuccessful body swerves, that's to say when you pretend you're going to turn right to make the defender think you're going to outflank him on the left, whereas in actual fact you *are* intending to pass him on the right, but your opponent, no doubt a descendant of those Vikings who used to sow terror in the Loire estuary in the IXth century before establishing themselves there, hence a big blond blood-drinker, doesn't bother his head with such strategic subtleties and unceremoniously shoulders you out of his way, calmly takes possession of the ball and boots it a long way back upfield with a feeling of having done his duty. The air of serene modesty he then adopts doesn't fool you: you can distinctly hear his head resounding with the cheers of a hundred-thousand-capacity stadium.

That's enough to upset anybody. The artist swept aside by brute force. And as if that wasn't enough of a lesson, your teammate, the one who got through the gap, lambasts you and, suiting the action to the word, raises his arms up to heaven, then drops them and, pointing to a clod of earth between his feet which doesn't really seem to be the matter at issue, informs you that he'd been there, on his own, simply waiting to be passed the ball so he could bury it – meaning, in the goal – and that he's fed up with all these splendid opportunites lost through your propensity to play solo, selfishly – that's the word – and that it really is a sign of extraordinary egotism when someone doesn't understand that a team game demands abnegation, co-operation, individuality subordinated to the group, and that in his opinion I would do better to spend my time playing darts, going fishing, or climbing a rope. But some murmurs, cutting short this all-against-one/all-for-one debate, inform you that the ball is already on its way back – it circulates at great speed in this type of game, from one end to the other like an undesirable stateless person – but now they're going to see what they're going to see, I'm going to trap it, that idiotic spherical object, under my foot. Now, trapping is an exercise that is much appreci-ated by our handful of supporters; they won't be able to deny your irreproachable technique, and it will make them regret all the more your alleged lack of interest in teamwork.

Whereas normally a ball bounces, this time, watch carefully, it's going to remain stuck to my boot. The foot, in suspension, gently accompanies the movement of the falling ball, thus reducing the force of resistance to zero. And the better to understand this physics problem, take two trains travelling in opposite directions on the same line. At the moment of the inevitable impact – horrible, but that's not the point – one of them begins to reverse and gradually halts the infuriated engine. Now, guess who plays the part of the virtuoso, the unflappable engine driver? You have only just solved this problem of the trains that cross without crossing when, taking advantage of your legitimate relaxation (you are mentally savouring the front page of the newspapers: he saves thousands of human lives, and the humble expression on your face in the full-page photo, eyelids lowered, I only did my duty), when suddenly and treacherously, from behind your back, up surges the blood-drinker and shoves his head between the ball and your boot. This time the two engines well and truly collide. Deafening sound of a shattered skull. But why doesn't he fall into a deep coma? For a moment you are petrified, your foot suspended above the ground juggling with an air bubble, amidst boos from the spectators and from the specialist of the gap: but what's he waiting for? The train? Your revenge will come shortly afterwards, your sweet consolation, the justification of your feeble effort: the vampire's forehead is dripping with mud. A quick look around tells me that I am the only one in this quagmire who isn't covered in mud. Which, in view of the conditions, is something of a miracle.

But I set great store by this two-bit luxury. It's my presumed distinction, my self-proclaimed elegance – like playing on freezing cold days with a scarf, which just happens to match the colour of my jersey, casually thrown round my neck. Showing off, they say. Above all, a way of showing, if you only knew, that I don't intend to cave in to you.

A few years earlier, mortified as one can be at thirteen, devastated by a defeat, miserable at not seeing my name on the team list, at a loss in the off season, I sometimes left the pitch without warning in the middle of a game, thus provoking the incomprehension of the other players, the referee, and the Sunday-morning volunteers, a thin crowd of fathers who had driven their sons to the ground and given a lift en route to the orphan waiting at the door of his mother's shop, bag in hand, for someone to come and pick him up, afraid they may have forgotten him, quite naturally getting into the back seat, the eternal passenger at the mercy of his hosts' timetables, gradually accustoming himself not to ask anybody for anything but to fend for himself, to refuse exeats, thus running the risk of severe reprimands. *Now* what's got into the boy? What had got into me was that I had a heavy cold, and had no wish to follow the common practice and blow my nose on my jersey, or, like some of the brasher ones, by closing one nostril with a finger, blowing very hard, and expelling a long trickle of snot which, before ramifying, indicated the direction of the wind, and whose remains were wiped with the back of your sleeve. An operation whose technique, being too timorous, I had never acquired, for in such a case what you have to do is lean forward, tilt your head three-quarters of the way round, forget your dignity and not do things by halves, for fear of the unfortunate conse-quences you can imagine. So the best thing to do was to run quickly and get a handkerchief from my things.

But that isn't done, no one's ever seen anything like it, why's he showing off again? And they drew my attention to this at the end of the match, back in the changing room – or what served as one – an old bus, for instance, its carcass towed goodness knows how to its graveyard, by a tractor no doubt – imagine the pride of the tractor hitched on to something other than its plough – , a customary type of recycling, like that of the van turned into a hen house at the bottom of a garden. Here, a Citroën bus, an ancient model you could still come across in the south of the department, chocolate-coloured metal and squashed bull-dog nose, flat tyres, broken windows replaced by green tarpaulins which immediately got slashed, likewise the seats, now oozing wadding and springs. But the essential remained: the big black Bakelite steering wheel, the pedals and gear lever, so there were always several boys fighting for their turn to play at being the driver.

But at that time any reprimand, however mild, such as: one doesn't abandon a game for such a frivolous reason, instantly filled my eyes with tears, obliging me to improvise a pathetic defence to stop them flowing, fighting to the last to find words, thinking: they're taking advantage of him not being here any more, if he was here, my father who died too soon, things wouldn't happen like this, and then, at a loss for arguments, picking on the coach of the little team, whose brief schooldays were long behind him, taking him up on a point of grammar – in the first place, you don't say this you say that – but the picked-on, a roadman by trade, staunch and loyal, restrained himself from slapping the face of the insolent picker-up, prevented, perhaps, by the still-fresh shadow of the great departed that came between them like a powerful wave rising from the depths.

Well then, think about it, to roll in the mud – unthinkable. Although it seems fairly obvious that it doesn't repel some, who leave the pitch even dirtier than a winner of the Paris–Roubaix bicycle race – the rainy years being the only ones that count in the legend of what is called the Northern Hell – with the colour of their jerseys no longer recognisable, to the point where you wonder how they manage not to go into the changing rooms by the wrong door, there being two of them (on one side the home team, on the other the visitors). But we should note that it's the mud-spattered ones that seem in less of a hurry to get under cover, that hang around to discuss strategy and technique, which is not without merit when you remember the confused mêlée, to analyse, to comment, thus giving their interlocutors time to admire their glorious wounds under their armour-plating of mud, until you begin to be afraid they might turn into human pottery if they were ever faced with any abrupt global warming – though that's hardly likely in these latitudes.

But in fact, no one can reproach them for a lack of combativity. The handful of supporters, always avid for blood, sweat and tears (although a little less so for tears), is full of praise for the courageous Resistance fighters and their innate knowledge of camouflage: their fierce determination to chase every ball, to hurl themselves between the feet of the opponent, to take every sort of punishment and give as good as they get, their refusal ever to admit defeat. All the more so as that's what we often are – defeated – it's our lot nearly every Sunday – and as it's not clear what is at stake. No hope of clawing our way up into the next division, no cup to win, not even the risk, given our rotten results, of being relegated, seeing that we're already in the very bottom category so there's nothing below us. The bedrock, that's us. Our sole objective is the desperate desire to be there, for lack of anywhere else to be. A rubbish-dump team, the reserve of the reserve, consisting of all the casualties of talent and the age limit: at eighteen you're too old for the youth team, at forty-five too pig-headed to admit that time has taken its toll.

The most admirable thing is that these maniacs of hand-to-hand combat sometimes manifest a kind of superior discouragement when they consider all their vain efforts, all the punishment they've taken without the consolation of victory, deploring in veiled terms the fact that some people don't play the game, at the same time casting a sidelong glance at the player who, as proof of his breach of faith, finished the game as clean as a whistle. Me, let's say. In fact, I am in no way responsible for the splashes on my thigh, it was an error ascribable to the hapless specimen who, no doubt the victim of a land-slip just at the crucial moment, aimed a violent kick at the ball, which missed, but encountered a clod of earth, thereby raising a shower of mud, a great deal of which descended on him, although those around him were not spared the odd imbruement. A blunder which, once he has cleaned up his eyes, he hastens to attribute to his defective studs; he checks the sole of his boot and, not discovering the fault, reties his lace, which is far too long, so sixty centimetres of it have to be wound round the ankle or instep, nevertheless it would never occur to anybody to shorten it, you would rather suggest docking the plume of a shako. And if the excuse of the boot doesn't seem accept-able, he still has the solution of limping for a few steps, putting his foot down on the ground very gingerly, the way you test the temperature of a hot plate with your hand, all the while displaying a grimace of pain under the mud mask. But he won't catch us like that again. From now on we avoid him like the plague. No question of getting into any sort of showdown with him. He can keep the ball, he can take his time, he can do whatever he likes, we're leaving the field open for him.

As for us, we play as we please, according to our mood, we try to avoid messing up our clothes and in all circum-stances to camouflage our effort, modelling ourselves on the fellow who sings while he's being tortured, or hums, or at least gives the impression that he's trying to remember a tune that escapes him, or again, taking as our model the lighthouse keeper who, although alone in his tower, still won't allow himself to crawl up the last hundred steps on all fours even though his only witnesses are the breakers hurling their luminous foam up on to the great stone Cyclops. The result, the end which is always too dreary to justify the means, is of less consequence to us than the beauty of the gesture. That's why, with my Indian cotton scarf round my neck, you see me, maybe without understanding, dribbling the puddles, skirting the molehills, those little volcanoes of loose earth knee-high to a grasshopper that are scattered all over fourth-rate football pitches, slaloming between the raindrops, making a present of a pass to an opponent, sending the ball straight into the arms of the rival goalkeeper, which saves him from wallowing in the mud – even if at this level we don't expect him to indulge in those spectacular flying leaps, those dolphin dives that are the delight of the Sunday-evening slow-motion replays on television, pictures shot light years away from an interstellar encounter between Mars and Jupiter. This goalkeeper is generally content to put out a hand, to extend a leg, or, if he thinks the shot is too violent, to protect his head with his folded arms and simply turn round and oppose his back and posterior, which sometimes present a surprising sight.

But these are the pretentions of an ineffectual aesthete which, understandably, raise the hackles of the spectators and the specialist of the gap. And yet that's all that is left to us, like women who, when they have nothing to look forward to on a certain day, spend the morning combing their eyelashes and painting their eyelids a vague shade of blue; that's all that is left to us on gloomy, damp, desolate Sundays, that's all: those little ballet-dancers' steps. Ballerinas' steps, as they say. If that amuses you.

THE FUNNIEST PART IS that I hadn't seen a thing – the wobbly vision of the myopic which keeps the world at a distance, confines it within a narrow perimeter of clarity whose contours become increasingly indistinct and powdery, beyond which shapes lose the rigidity of their lines, slide into a loose-fitting sheath, are surrounded by a kind of electronic cloud. Which constitutes a physical, or rather a scientific, reality, so that the myope is left with a microscopic view of things and can even detect the filament of the lachrymal liquid moving over his retina.

But when it comes to the macroscopic – just a short distance away from the iris it's an athanor: the universe fuses, disintegrates, becomes a fuzzy, blurrred, Verlainian domain, a tachist landscape composition, its colours sloshing all over the place, its volumes watercoloured, its masses misty, its perspective evanescent, its depth flattened, its outlines indistinct, its Michelin-man clouds deflated, the sky hangs like a theatre backdrop, electric lights are swamped in a maze of micro-sparks, the sun becomes corpuscular, the moon's disc haloed, whatever the season, by a paraselene, that chalky corona people say is a sign of snow. Well, no – and this is the good news – it may be a lovely day tomorrow. This is the way we learn how to dispense with the advice of weather forecasters, futurologists, clairvoyants. Days reveal themselves one by one, as they come. What's the use of preparing for them in advance? Tomorrow will take care of itself. When it comes to foretelling in obscure quatrains the cataclysms and plagues of the year three thousand, we myopes, on account of our vision being knee-high to the daisies, fall a little short, being too preoccupied with trying to see what is staring us in the face, but for anything to do with the life of the ants, once we get our noses down in the grass, nothing escapes us. The art of detail, the rustle of the wind, the pitter-patter of the rain – these are our stock in trade.

As for the middle distance, the foggy zone, the most awkward of all, that's a question of method. Take, for example, that green dome suspended above the ground. In a fraction of a second (you see how it makes the brain agile and deductive), you eliminate the possibility of a monumental cupola, like Saint Peter's in Rome, the Invalides, the Val-de-Grâce, which is generally covered in gold leaf; or of a flying saucer, which comes in the shape of a saucer; or of a cloud of poison gas (war hasn't been declared); therefore it must be a tree. You approach it. Bravo. For further information you jump up and pluck a leaf, you study it: lobed edges, virtual absence of petiole – therefore it's a pedunculate oak. Would you learn as much if you were lynx-eyed? And then, and this is no secret for anyone, all the things in this world have so often been depicted, described, analysed, exhibited, shown from every angle, that no one even bothers to look at them any more. People think they know them by heart. Humming a merry little tune, they swear in good faith that that is Paris, whereas Paris isn't that any more, or at least not quite that any more, it's already something else. Paris would have to be ruined, devastated, razed to the ground, before it occurred to them to add a nostalgic couplet, and even then not immediately. Retinal persistence. But we will admit that this reduced vision does have its drawbacks. To hear you talk, we can never so much as get a sniff at a beautiful panorama. Maybe not, but what do you do with a beautiful panorama? Do you enjoy it? Really enjoy it? You're having me on. In any case, we have the *View of Delft*, and if we are to believe *Impression, Rising Sun*, we aren't missing much.

On the pitch, the ball, even when it's done a vanishing act, can be located fairly easily. In an arid, desolate place, when your attention is caught by the sight of vultures circling overhead, you casually look up and say: ah, a corpse. It's the same thing here. The ball is where there's the greatest concentration of players. And anyway, it's always the hide of that tragic old goat that is fought over, that's to say not so much its stylised carcass as its superpowers. And it's true that no one would ever have made such a song and dance about a monogamous goat: as a result, no Abraham, no Greek drama, no football games. Dismal Sundays. And from time to time, provided it isn't too far away, you approach that human bundle, the way you up go to an information desk, out of curiosity, just to see, to set your mind at rest, but sometimes, surprise surprise, the crowd has gathered round a man on the ground, howling with pain and holding his leg. *A priori*, that's nothing to get excited about, it's quite a customary scene, and yet it's in such cases that dodgy vision can play tricks on you. Before you accuse the injured man of shamming and urge him to cut the comedy and get back on his feet pronto, you should check that his tibia doesn't happen to be sticking out at a right angle. This might turn out to be embarrassing – and not only for the injured party.

However, most of the time it doesn't do any good to run: wait for it to come to you. There will always be a moment during the match when the ball will land at your feet. Either because in an excess of zeal you have claimed it, and a skilful and altruistic teammate thought it would be an act of charity to pass it to you (or, not knowing what to do with it, had decided to get rid of it by passing it to you), or because fate had taken matters in hand and, as a result of a formidable calculation of probability, it so happens that it's your turn to play.

My turn to play? All right, but just tell that specialist of the gap, that eternal conqueror of the opposite defence, just tell him to stop yelling and demanding the ball. Everybody needs something, we all have a right to amuse ourselves. For, as things stand, you don't get much of a chance to see the ball during a match – and I with my dioptric problems even less so – he ought to understand that, and be a good sport. Fate, with the ball bouncing unpredictably along aleatory trajectories, has so decided: it's my turn; his will come. His frantic dashes behind the opposing defence line are sure to bear fruit in the end (this is what he calls "playing the English game", a rather rough and ready tactic, incidentally: long balls upfield, sprinters racing up to the goal line, until you can't tell any more whether they're playing children's playground games, or are pondering that mathematical problem in which someone rather lacking in common sense picks up an apple every metre and takes it back to his basket every time, thus covering a distance the equivalent of three times round the planet, which, for a compote, a bowlful of cider or a Tarte Tatin, does somewhat complicate life).

But, now that you have the ball at your feet, the question arises: what do you do with it? The ideal would be to keep it for the rest of the game, to keep it there like a pet dog, but that's unheard of. One day it might well be heard of, but if ever some admirable fellow were to take it upon himself to represent the whole corps de ballet on his tod, I wouldn't much care to be in his shoes. So the best thing is to feint. For example, by passing it to someone on your side, expecting him to send it back to you. This is called a one-two, and it's a figure that is also appreciated by the handful of supporters. But as you're never sure of seeing your ball again (your mate isn't necessarily inspired by the same sentiments where you are concerned), you might just as well hang on to it. The trouble is that you then have a whole horde hot on your heels. With the aggression they sometimes manifest, anyone might think they were launched on a manhunt. So you do your best to outmanoeuvre the traps they set for you, their out-stretched legs, their less than friendly shoves, their elbows in your ribs, their tugs at your shirt. You whirl, you whiz round like a bee shut up in a bottle, you look for the weak point in this human labyrinth. Usually you retreat – and all this jiggling and juggling is totally unproductive – but the ball, which is what matters and is why you're there, remains firmly stuck under your foot. You don't take your eyes off it; your head obstinately lowered, you are imper-vious to the protests of this one and that. You build yourself a cone of existence, its vertex being the source of your gaze, its base being the limit the ball must not cross. Which, naturally, if you are to believe them, is the exact opposite of what you're supposed to do. How can you assess the game, anticipate, prepare future combi-nations, if you have your nose stuck in your boots? But they're just preaching to themselves, that lot, in favour of what they want to see. And what do they know about the perspective of the visually challenged?

When I was between twelve and fifteen, my golden age,

it was not unusual for four or five of them to have a go at me to try to block me. You think I'm exaggerating, that I'm taking advantage of the situation, but not really, and that's how you get a minor reputation for being a scarecrow. But what remains of it a few years later, after a long sabbatical leave? Bodies have become filled out, have doubled in volume, have grown three heads taller. Will-o'-the-wisps, subjected to the same process yet still chasing the living flame of childhood, at the mercy of this brutal metamorphosis, blown hither and thither, are inevitably snuffed out, their delicate Mozartian music drowned by the municipal brass band. The new order escapes them. The big blond, who landed from his Viking long ship and was warned of the bitterness of existence, doesn't burden himself with these refinements, affectations, fioriture. The perspective shrinks, as do the pleasures of the myopic.

It isn't the thing any longer, this art of the pirouette. So just one last song, one last little dance step: a sudden swerve to the right, a sideways move to the left, flip the ball, which bounces back on to the toe of your boot, and, with your back to the goal, by guesswork, because you don't really know where it is, a long way away no doubt, much too far for my striking force, suddenly turn round and kick the ball, the way you dismiss your childhood which has disappeared into the remote, hazy distance. And that would be it, if, to your amazement, you didn't suddenly see the fists of your teammates punch the air in triumph. You hear the referee's whistle, a sort of shrill cooing sound, the flattering murmurs of the supporters on the touchline congratulating themselves that their good advice – shoot, but why doesn't he shoot? – has finally borne fruit, and you realise that, unknown to you, the ball must have managed to insinuate itself between the keeper and the uprights. You will never know exactly where – the top corner, maybe, hence the flattering murmurs – nor whether the nets shook, but, joining – somewhat out of synch – in the jubilation of the aficionados, you too punch the air with a conquering fist. You tell yourself, no doubt, that it's a pity not to be a spectator of your own exploits. Not a bit of it. You are the one and only witness of something infinitely more subtle: a secret little smile from destiny.

THE MARK HAD BY now practically disappeared, all that remained after several weeks was a vague memory of a bruised shoulder, but the friendly pats of my habitual denigrators, congratulating me on my formidable blind goal, contributed to its revival. And if I smiled it wasn't, as they thought, because of my exploit which, as I was not unaware, was essentially due to chance, to the wind, and to the lack of skill of the opposing goalkeeper. I was smiling because for several Sundays now I had been the fellow sitting on the bench, bare-chested, bending over his sports bag searching at length for his shirt or for an unlikely tube of ointment, hoping that someone would finally notice the stigma on his left shoulder and follow up with a suggestive, or even bawdy, comment, which would have left no doubt about the origin of the scar. But no one, not even Gyf, with whom I had played one or two trial matches before they relegated me to the rubbish-dump team, had noticed a thing, so, piqued, I finally got dressed without even bothering to wash, or maybe just a lick and a promise.

No question indeed of having a communal shower, of exhibiting oneself, like some of them who, having soaped themselves vigorously, hang around without apparent embarrassment in a state of nature, treating you to an account of a fascinating strategic phase of the game, while you plunge your head into your bag in search of the unlikely ointment. You might have thought they would take advantage of the situation by advancing other arguments, but no, seen from the bottom of my bag, nothing to get alarmed about, and I certainly agreed that after what I had just shown them, that historic goal, I ought to try my luck from a distance more often, but there, on my shoulder, can't you see anything? That dentate halo profoundly embedded in the skin, doesn't that mean anything to you? You know the story of Cinderella's slipper and her tiny foot? Well, if you were to try out all the dentitions in the world (to simplify: of the feminine sex, around twenty years old, and registered as living in this region), there is only one that would correspond exactly with this impression. For your guidance, and for the pleasure it gives me to pronounce her name, the beauty with the ferocious bite calls herself Theo. But Theo: you simply can't imagine. So go and exhibit your wrinkled little whatsit elsewhere.

Or perhaps it was that they couldn't bring themselves to make me a present of a word, of a remark, that would have elevated me in their eyes to the status of a man. And yet, over the weeks, the bite had gradually evolved through all the colours of the rainbow, from red to blue, from yellow to violet, and was only now returning to something resembling the colour of normal flesh and becoming not much more than a memory. So the hands pummelling my shoulder by way of paying tribute to my talents as a scorer, in reviving this wound that was well on its way to a cure, came, like a booster injection, as a sharp reminder of my night of love.

Theo hadn't taken me by surprise; she had warned me, even before she started on my shoulder, that I shouldn't hesitate to stop her if I thought she was making too free with me, but I had seen it as a sort of Ordeal, a sort of divine judgment, and I would have let her peel off my flesh rather than beg for mercy. Which she would no doubt have done if she hadn't achieved satisfaction. After which, she deposited a chaste restorative kiss on the same spot, merely enquiring: it didn't hurt? What are you talking about, sweet Theo? while I check with my fingertips that blood is not flowing from my shoulder.

Gyf had been somewhat discouraged by the reception of his speech at the General Meeting, during which the discussion of the final wording of the slogans for the demonstration had forced him into a perilous verbal sparring match. The criticisms of the comrade students, who hadn't appreciated the authoritarian way he took the floor, even claiming that he was a crypto-conservative, not to say a stooge of high international finance (he, a poor orphan, and the only genuine Mongo-Aoustinian of the group), had cooled his revolutionary ardour and, distancing himself a little from the cause, he had opportunely remembered that even without militancy he was not short of interests.

As organiser, in his grandmother's village, of the Logréean Club, he had taken it into his head, no doubt as a reaction (those same comrades accusing him of opiumising the people), to play at being a recruiting sergeant. So, after we met again, he had got into the habit of visiting me in my room at the hall of residence, where, over the beers he kindly brought with him, he informed me of his multifarious projects, never at any time omitting to remind me that he still counted on me to compose the music for his film. But to tell the truth it was a one-way conversation, which interested him all the more in that he had found the ideal listener in me. Even though he had one day caught a glimpse on my desk of a few extracts from my great work, a play about a kind of double of Rimbaud, dealing with his impossible return, he had never had the curiosity to ask me anything about it. From which I had realised, sadly but gratefully, that Theo was the only person who had ever shown any real interest in my Jean-Arthur who, when deprived of his one and only female adorer, had lapsed into a cryogenic coma in which he would wait until the end of time for the beauty to come and release him.

For to tell the truth, if I lent such a benevolent ear to Gyf's logorrhoea, it was only because I was hoping to come across Theo in it, to find out a bit more about her, about what had become of her, or even just to hear her name. But he only once alluded to her, and then briefly, when he asked me whether I had seen her since the demonstration and, as I answered in the negative, not wishing to enter into any confidences, he didn't press the point, preferring to remember, while we were talking about Saint-Cosmes and our recollections of school, that I wasn't at all bad when I had a ball between my feet. If his memory served him aright, I was even quite difficult to check: did I still play? Not for two or three years, why did he ask? Well, if I didn't know what to do with my Sundays, he suggested he might put my name down for the Club; Logrée wasn't all that far from Random and he would come and collect me, it would be a good opportunity for us to meet outside the university.

The snag was that I wasn't sure I would still be as interested in it as before, which anyway was the reason I stopped playing. As the players get older the game gets rougher and rougher, too rough for the nimble-footed specialists of the filigree, of the subtly wiggling hips, of fancy choreography. You find yourself back in the spirit of the school playground: the toughs in defence and the little ones – me, obviously – the wing forwards, that's to say the ones who get driven on to the touchline by the big hulking ones. So you can well imagine what an unequal struggle it is between the little pirouetting guy and the great big pushing and shoving one. It's always the same old story, Gyf. You only have to remember the famous naval battle in the Gulf of Morbihan between the Venetian sailing ships and the Roman galleys. Now who won, I ask you? And who was responsible for that tragedy? Caesar? No, it was the wind, the wind that never stops blowing here, on the shores of the ocean, and which, almost as if it did it on purpose, let us down that evening. True, it does just occasionally drop at the close of the day, but that wasn't the day for it to choose. And just when it looked as if the battle was going to swing in favour of the Atlantic, suddenly not a breath of air, the sails flap and droop like empty goatskins, causing an abrupt halt to the ballet of the canvas insects which, only a moment before, were making monkeys of the powerful galleys, amusing themselves by brushing up against them, letting fly a broadside of arrows in passing, and then exploiting the next gust of wind to make their escape. And while the Armoricans vainly scru-tinise the motionless sky, you can already hear the ferocious rhythm of the oars slashing through the mirror of the water, making a beeline for the fishing boats becalmed between the islands. You can well imagine that that lot didn't give a damn for their gods, so, rather than praying to Aeolus, they simply relied on the strength of their arms. But from that point on, there's no more to be said. Any minute now – just long enough for the men of Rome to launch their grappling irons and close in along-side the rival boats – any minute now, the hand-to-hand fighting on those improvised rings, opposing on the one side the technique of militarism and on the other the science and knowledge of the winds and tides, just one more minute of indecision during which they pretend to believe that all is not lost, but as night falls on the still waters that have retreated towards the great menhir in Locmariaquer, as the fine drizzle falls on the foreheads of the conquered, lying in the blue sludge besmirched with pink puddles, while the clamour of the legionaries is heard rising in the oceanic night, that's the end of the proud independence of the Atlantic mariners. And we all know what came out of that: hot baths, short swords, and Latin declensions – rosa, a rose. I don't need to spell it out for you, Gyf. It's infuriating, though. Brute force always wins; methodical, organised force. All it leaves for the light cavalry is miserable, unimportant, provisional victories – which are not so much victories, actually, as exercises in style, pirouettes.

Gyf was not entirely sure that he had taken all this in, nor how the defeat of the Venetians had influenced my reluctance to re-enlist for duty on the football pitch. Or maybe I had been trying to demonstrate that the victories of Italian players in the various European and World competitions had their origin in the dim and distant past. But as the prospect of some form of entertainment, however pathetic, for my dismal Sundays made me think twice about turning down his suggestion out of hand, he managed to find the right arguments to overcome my resistance. As I balked at submitting to the formalities, he promised me that he would take care of everything, the signatures and the fake medical certificates, and that all he needed were two passport photos for which he couldn't replace me (just as well, at that, because Gyf's glasses . . .). But with such methods, anyone can get more or less anything he likes out of me, such as making me wear the green shirt with the blue collar of the Logréean Club (thanks to which we were greeted with resounding quack-quacks when we ran on to the pitch), even though I don't really want to, but just because I have nothing better to do, and, in a pathetic sort of way, to alleviate my solitude.

On the strength of my past exploits, Gyf had announced me as the saviour who was going to get the *Logréean Canards* promoted to the next division, so for my first appearances the public had doubled, kind of from four to eight. But already neither the first muttered comments nor the circumspect expressions of the handful of connoisseurs registered any obvious enthusiasm: without wishing to make too hasty a judgment of his gifts, didn't the messiah seem just that bit fragile? When he has the ball, that's to say when he has been presented with it on a plate, it isn't that he doesn't know what to do with it, no doubt he would be perfect in a circus, but all his juggling acts don't lead to anything very much except to give the ball back to the opponent, and this apparently in the great evangelical tradition in which, rather than claim eye and tooth for eye and tooth, you prefer to turn the other cheek, but that after all is not the goal, the goal is the goal. Where is he, then, the saviour who, in three days, in his own way, was supposed to be going to rebuild the glorious temple of the exploits of the Club?

Gyf had done too much, said too much. Their disappointment was commensurate with the hopes he had raised. But they decided they ought to give me a little time, time to acclimatise myself, to get to know my teammates and to familiarise myself with their method of play. So they gave me a second chance the following Sunday.

But this wasn't much more convincing, in spite of Gyf, who had gone rushing around like a blue-arsed fly, covering the whole pitch, his long hair streaming behind him or swirling in front of his eyes, in order to send me as many balls as possible, thus delivering me up to the condemnation of our comrades who bemoaned all the great opportunities wasted by my propensity to play on my own.

At the same time, it was strange to observe Gyf, how little he had changed. He already used to play like that at Saint-Cosmes, he was inexhaustible, and what had amused us at the time was his perpetual-motion, busy-bee side, always backing lost or hopeless causes – as for instance sprinting after a ball that everyone knew was going out – which now paid off handsomely, and it was I, the former juggler, who became the laughing stock, so much so that I had to console him when they informed me that from now on I would have to prove myself in the reserve team. It was as if the last traces of his childhood had vanished when his memory played him false.

As a result I lost my chauffeur, who could no longer come and pick me up since the two teams played on different grounds, so I had to go to Logrée on my Vélosolex. From there, if we were playing an away match I got a lift with a player or spectator, thus reverting to the old habits I had liked to believe had gone for ever. I was still the orphan, the underprivileged, fatherless boy dependent on other people's goodwill.

The two of us who didn't have a driving licence were waiting by the Café des Sports for someone to be so good as to give us a lift: La Fouine – the Weasel – a little man, more or less the village idiot, and me. The fact of our mutual membership of the brotherhood of those unsuited for modern life brought us together by force of circumstance: would there be room for the two idiots? In any case, he came into that category almost officially. If he didn't drive, at least he had an excuse, for he could neither read nor write, or only just; he used to await confirmation before entering his team's cloakroom, in case he gave the two balls he was responsible for to the opponents.

These two balls were his pride and joy. And although they were no longer needed, leather by then being coated in plastic, he used to take them home with him and grease them with some stuff that made them shine like the sun in the string bag he carried on his back, which made him look like a little hunchback when he covered them with the big green cape that hung down to his feet. For he couldn't have been more than four foot six, with his weight in proportion. When I asked him whether he had a Christian name, because it embarrassed me to call him by his nickname, he refused point blank and insisted: Me, I'm La Fouine; ever since I was very little, La Fouine here, La Fouine there, hee hee, everyone knows La Fouine, hee hee, and then he would scrunch himself up even smaller, tucking his head into his shoulders, bending his knees, as if he was trying to show that he could squeeze himself through a mousehole. So, as he was so keen on his nickname, I wasn't going to upset him, and the result was that the day he came to Random my mother greeted him with a bonjour Monsieur La Fouine, which absolutely delighted him. If he is still alive, that's to say if he is still polishing his two footballs, he is certainly still talking about it: Just think, Monsieur La Fouine, hee hee, while straightening an imaginary knot in his tie to smarten himself up, and he used to insist on the players addressing him as Monsieur La Fouine before he would hand over the balls, which got him snubbed twice as much as usual, so the very least I could do, in the name of our brotherhood, was entrust him with my violin.

He hugged it tight all through the match, standing on the touchline jealously defending it against the inquisitive, who suggested he should take it out of its case and let them see what it looked like, and then hugging it even more tightly as if it were an infinitely precious object, or a child he was keeping warm under his jacket, and he would have died on the spot rather than let go of it. To people who yelled at him: Come on, La Fouine, aren't you going to blow into your instrument for us? he responded that what *they* needed was to blow into a bag, or else: Hey, La Fouine, so you've brought your machine gun to make off with the takings, to which his response, pointing the case at the foolhardy joker, was: You'd better not come any closer, or daca-daca-dac! So it had given him both importance and wit and when, at the end of the game, after my victorious goal, he clung on to my painful shoulder with his free hand, he was joy personified, with the tufts of his hair sticking up on top of his head making him look like an imitation Stan Laurel, and he cried: It was the violin that brought you luck, hee hee, you were quite right to leave it with me, hee hee, it was the violin, and, tucking the case, which was almost as big as him, under his chin, he began to dance a kind of jig, jerking his short legs up one after the other like a puppet, advancing a few steps, retreating as many, all the time nodding his head: You'll have to bring it every Sunday, we'll get them dancing, hee hee, they'll see what they'll see, all the time spraying the pitch with an imaginary salvo.

II

I‌f it hadn't been for Gyf, I don't suppose anyone would ever have seen me on a football pitch again. Such improbable reversions are a bad sign. With rare exceptions: Racine, perhaps, twelve years after *Phèdre*, but on the sly, with the plays he wrote for the convent schoolgirls of Saint-Cyr. If it hadn't been for Gyf, and the solitude of my Sundays. For whatever you do, Sundays are almost always disappointing, which is enough to make you wonder whether there wasn't a design fault from the very beginning, whether there wasn't something hidden behind that offer of a day of rest after six days of sweated labour. Hence the Gyfian aphorism: when the bosses start suggesting presents of that sort, infernal rates of production are never very far away.

During the week, though, from the boarders' point of view, we waited for Sunday as if it were a promise of salvation. The electric bells that regulated the life of the school – the beginning and end of lessons, recreation breaks, meals, bedtime – only signalled release at five o'clock on Saturdays. And there was no question of any slacking beforehand under the pretext that we were beginning to see the end of the tunnel. Some teachers even took great pleasure in going into extra time after the bell. And woe betide anyone who, by a pronounced sigh, a cough, or merely a glance at his watch, took it into his head to indicate that the timetable had been overrun. Disciplinary action followed instantly: homework for the ill-mannered pupil and ten minutes longer for the whole class – which meant that some were likely to miss the bus, and others the ferry that shuttled between the banks of the estuary. (The latter, on stormy days, also had to keep an anxious eye on the state of the sea, on which the crossing depended.)

Gyf, who was the most insolent, and hence the most courageous, of us all, one day responded to this repeated delay by ostentatiously doing up his schoolbag and, braving the professorial wrath, getting up and marching out, slamming the door. Naturally, he already knew that he was going to be expelled at the end of the school year (he was only at Saint-Cosmes for one year, the first), but it showed amazing panache. And it was also very funny. Because before slamming the door he launched a paper aeroplane across the classroom on which he had written something like shit to the person who reads this – which the principal authority didn't fail to do, after having confiscated and unfolded the said aeroplane. Facing him were thirty faces, terrorised at the idea of not being able to prevent themselves from bursting out laughing. What was he supposed to do? We were kept in for a further ten minutes.

This was why we were wary of Gyf's outbursts. Before applauding, we waited until we had been presented with the bill for the whole class. This didn't show a great deal of solidarity with him, but we were so punch-drunk with victimisation of all sorts that we avoided adding to them. And then, we told ourselves that he had found his role, that he was playing it to the hilt and deriving prestige from it; a splendid, flattering and awesome role, in spite of its risks. This figure of the hero, of the school bandit, naturally had its price in the punishments he received, sometimes physical (he took slaps in the face without batting an eyelid, and much better than did his glasses, which eventually, being the type that is reimbursed in full by the Social Security and not exactly beautiful, presented a curious asymmetry, the left-hand lens being wedged into his eye-socket like a monocle). But that, after all, was more enviable than being in the skin of a trembling little boy, so timorous that when fate sent him up to the blackboard he addressed a prayer to heaven and, under the pretext of attenuating a cough in the hollow of his hand, surreptitiously kissed the baptismal medal hanging round his neck.

The said blackboard was in fact green, which contributed a modern note nicely in keeping with the twin buildings of the school – tall, cream-coloured concrete façades, wide openings, semi-circular gables, flat roofs – enclosing the little single-storeyed house, in the centre of which was a rectangular porch protected by the bars of a green gate, that was used as the caretaker's lodge and constituted the main entrance. Postwar architecture, the same as at Saint-Nazaire, Le Havre, Brest, Royan, Lorient, the bombed-out ports now completely rebuilt, with their rectilinear avenues in which the wind gets trapped. Saint-Cosmes, standing along the seafront, thus took on the appearance of a holiday home for gilded schoolboys. Which prevented us from complaining: it was hard to explain, given such conditions, that inside the building the mentalities of another century had survived the Anglo-Saxon raids.

A blackboard has a constricted, obscurantist, Manichaean side to it, whereas that springlike rectangle on the wall near the desk, above the dais, seemed to authorise some liberties with the law, for instance that the sum of the angles of a triangle was more or less equal to two right angles. But it was that more or less, that guilty indecision, that brought us the worst humiliations. If the reply didn't come out rapidly and correctly, then a cruel game began in which we very soon saw who was playing the cat and who the mouse. While the mouse – me, since there has to be a victim – scared stiff, brows knitted, chalk hovering, pondered, doing his best to pile up all the fictitious angles of a dismantled triangle, all the time considering that if an angle is bigger or smaller, three bigger or smaller angles add up to a bigger or smaller angle, the cat – but we may as well call him Monsieur Fraslin – losing patience, grabbed the big wooden dividers for use on the board and, instead of doing what was probably necessary and replacing the chalk which was held in a copper grip surrounded by a sliding ring, ostentatiously tested the sharpness of the point with the tip of his finger.

This time, however, I was not told to draw a circle, I was put to the question, in the sense in which that phrase was understood in the gaols of the Middle Ages, which is to say that Inquisitor Fraslin – one of the rare laymen in this cassock-clad menagerie, who had a long brown strand of hair falling over his forehead which he used to toss back with a nervous movement of his head, who was given to sidelong glances, who was lanky and bony, and whose trousers concertinaed over his ankles – took a cigarette lighter out of his pocket, ignited it, held the point of the open dividers in the flame, heated it with meticulous care, turning it round and round like a spit, and, now that its pathogenic germs had been destroyed and that all risk of infection had been removed, armed with this anti-septic lance he amused himself by pricking the bottom of the back of the recalcitrant mathematician, although no one ever knew whether he was punishing his ignorance or attempting in this way to sharpen his mental faculties.

Actually, this operation was less painful than embarrassing, but it was truly embarrassing, because of the laughter of your classmates who imagined that it would meet with approval and maybe allow them to avoid the next massacre – as if their turn wasn't going to come. With your thoughts becoming increasingly confused and entirely concentrated on the next assault, you pretended to be pondering while you gazed out of the wide windows behind which great big white birds with silver wings were floating, free, without a care in the world, playing in the wind, emitting excited little cries, surfing on the airstreams, soaring on an ascending flux, suddenly becoming motionless, their vibrant feathers poised in suspension against the blue background of the sky, then, dipping a wing, sideslipping, and disappearing out of the window frame, leaving the huge, profound sky without a solution. So as a last resort you sent a questioning look at your seated friends, the unfortunate laughers, trying to read a hint of an answer on the lips of an omniscient one, but they also were too frightened, and Gyf probably didn't know.

And when you are at such a complete and utter loss, there is nothing for it but to write a random figure on the board, which is immediately disapproved of by the point of the dividers. Why not 1515? says the picador, suiting the action to the words. You hurriedly erase the error with the felt brush, raising a cloud of chalk. Suddenly, an inspiration: if every triangle is inscribable within a circle, the sum of its angles must be less than 360°. Mustn't make a mistake and use the inequality sign – a V on its side. Remember: the smaller eats the bigger. That's good thinking. Irrefutable? Not really. This time the prick is so sharp that you knock your head against the board. General hilarity. And that makes you laugh? All the exercises on page 127 to be given in by tomorrow. Serves them right, you think. Yes, but. For you, on top of that, a hundred lines: the sum of the angles of a triangle is equal to two right angles.

THESE HUMILIATING TITILLATIONS WERE not for Gyf who, in view of his rank and his service record, enjoyed preferential treatment, which was at the same time more indulgent and more violent. This was only fair, because honestly we couldn't stand comparison with him. Whereas he, from his twelve- or thirteen-year-old height, might brazenly look the authorities of the establishment up and down, we had to content ourselves, in the acts-of-resistance category, with half-pulling a face behind the back of a supervisor, and even then with a hand over our mouth and our head lowered. And if this supervisor, the cunning devil, smelling a rat, suddenly turned round in order to catch the novice rebel in the act, even before he had said anything, we hastily specified: I didn't do anything, m'sieur, or better still, and to be more convincing: It wasn't me, m'sieur. Which seems like nothing, or perhaps nothing much, but this participation, however timid, prevented us from remaining tongue-tied at Gyf's exploits and allowed us too to have our word to say, on the principle that all things are equal, that we also had shown courage – as much as we were capable of, of course – and that in any case it's the intention that counts.

After that, we had the nerve to interrupt him half way through his stories with something of the order of: Just like me . . . Whereas he, for zero plus zero equals zero, might have drawn on the board a "Toto's head" (that extremely stylised head where the two zeros represent the eyes, the plus sign the nose, and the equals sign the mouth, the whole inscribed within a circle), Just-like-me had stolen a piece of chalk that had fallen on to the ground, by kicking it, after the end of the class, to the door, and there had bent down and picked it up under the pretext of doing up his schoolbag, which entailed a double risk: one, of being spotted, with the terrible consequences you are aware of, and two, of crushing the chalk, hence the importance of knowing how to dribble and the advantage of a subtle touch with the ball, which not everybody can boast of (Gyf's speciality on a football pitch was chasing after every ball; inexhaustible, but of limited technique), don't you want to believe me? (He doesn't want anything, doesn't say anything, he's just simply flabbergasted by this frog pretending to be an ox, who is a great deal less of a braggart in the presence of the authorities), well then, look, and the piece of chalk comes out of the bigmouth's pocket, together with an ink-stained handkerchief and a few lumps of sugar, and is brandished under his nose like Exhibit A. How about that, then?

After the ceiling lights – white globes similar to the ones in our family shop – were put out at half past eight, it wasn't unusual for the only boy not in bed to be Gyf, kneeling on the cold, tiled floor of the somnolent dormitory, facing the wall, near the supervisor, whose silhouette we could see like a Chinese shadow through the cream-coloured curtains of his canvas bedsit. Sitting at his table, reading under the dome of his bedside light, which was deliberately subdued so as not to disturb the sleepers (his attitude was a continuing source of wonder to us: but how could he possibly study by the side of a suffering humiliated child?), this vigilante took a visible delight in making us believe he had eyes in the back of his head, and also in reprimanding the kneeler every time he tried to sit back on his heels on the sly, which made us think that he was only pretending to be absorbed in his book, and that he was less fascinated by his studies than by his discretionary power. And so while Gyf, on his knees, had endured this man's cruelty for two whole hours, with the occasional show of rebellion – which automatically entailed a prolongation of his torture, Just-like-me, taking advantage of the semi-darkness (for night in the dormitory is a clear night and, even after Cerberus has put out his nightlight, the street lamps along the seafront cast a lunar glow which filters through the imperfectly closed heavy green curtains) – Just-like-me had not hesitated to thumb an avenging nose – with his head under the sheets, it's true – at the cruel supervisor, to make very clear his disagreement with the punishment that had befallen his friend. And Gyf was expected to show his gratitude for this heroic demonstration, and to agree that this obscure resistance had prompted the torturer, a couple of hours later, to send him back to bed.

In this way, without appearing to be unduly worried, he brought down on his head an accumulation of hours of detention, of kilometres of lines to write (you will do me a hundred lines, which he rarely did), of occasions when he was sent out of the room (they were never sure of finding him when the moment came for him to be allowed back in), of visits to the master in charge of discipline (nick-named Juju, who wasn't the worst of the gang in spite of his severe look, which was essentially caused by his roving right eye. This eye was always casting sidelong glances at the seagulls while the other one was lecturing you, so you sometimes wondered what possible reprehensible act it could have committed, that laughing seagull, with its red beak and brown head hooded like the Butcher of Béthune, to deserve to be kept in for two hours – its mocking cry wrongly interpreted, no doubt – but this act of injustice is soon rectified, *listen* to me when I'm talking to you, so the seagull is innocent, *you* are the guilty party) not forgetting, apart from the victimisation and the deprival of Sunday exeats – which Gyf pretended he couldn't care less about, being an adopted child, or perhaps simply living with foster-parents. But his endurance impressed his persecutors who, also taking his family situation into account, sometimes showed him surprising indulgence.

IN THIS QUASI-MONASTIC WORLD, silence was naturally the rule except in the playground and refectory – but there we still had to wait until a sort of grace had been said, in the vernacular: For what we are about to receive, Lord make us truly thankful, to which, standing behind our chairs, arms folded, would-be devout expressions on our faces, we replied Amen, although Gyf changed the "what" into "this shit" (it must be admitted, apart from the blasphemous aspect, that the food wasn't all that great). Then, energetically clapping his hands, the aforementioned Juju would give the seagulls permission – although, without being sure, we took it that it was also intended for us – to sit down and start yakking. Not too loudly, though. The spectre of an uproar with salvos of fromage blanc, volleys of purée and other missiles, which we contented ourselves with miming, a full spoon transformed into a trebuchet aimed at a classmate or at the ceiling globe, with one's middle finger pressing on the edge of the spoon and acting as the relief-valve, involved keen vigilance and frequent calls to order whenever the noise level, reflected back by the wide glass windows and the tiled floor, was in danger of becoming a real brouhaha. Once more, hands were clapped, even more energetically than the first time, prompting us to lower the volume, or even, in case of a subsequent offence, condemning us to silence until the end of the meal, a silence which was nevertheless broken by the clatter of knives and forks, of plates being piled up and glasses being banged down. Curiously enough, it was not Gyf who always took the occasion to belch loudly in this Cistercian atmosphere, it was a boy who tended to be a model of discretion, but who found such situations a fertile breeding ground for his remarkable capacity to produce this kind of sound on demand. Collective, liberating laughter, all the more confident because in the refectory we weren't afraid of retaliatory measures against the whole group. It was only the sound-effects engineer, long since detected, who copped the ritual hundred lines: I will not engage in such unseemly acts in the future, whereupon the said perpetrator retorted every time, and all the X-rays showed it was true, that he suffered from aerophagia. And he lost no time in lifting up his shirt to exhibit his famous air pocket, the source of all his woes, but that wasn't what they wanted, they simply required him to put his hand over his mouth, and therefore the hundred lines were doubled. Which, for this moment of glory, was practically dirt cheap.

In class, this kind of demonstration was unthinkable. As for opening one's mouth, one had to wait to be invited to do so by the competent authority – but this was rarely a good sign. The masters never picked on anyone who was expected to know – if he knows, what's the use of asking him? And that is precisely what worries him, the one who does know, always the same one, this knowledge which he never manages to parade in public but from which he hopes to get something more than an appreciative comment at the top of his essay, because that is merely personal, almost intimate – he would like his manifest superiority to be trumpeted abroad. Which means that he sometimes forgets to put up his hand, he can't wait to come out with the right answer, and he's so exasperated by the lack of culture of the boy sitting next to him that he gets to the point of snapping his fingers: a sharp click of his thumb against his middle finger intended to draw attention to himself, although he should know, poor wretch, that it is quite obvious that the authority, from the height of his dais, is deliberately, very deliberately, ignoring him. So much so that this insistence, this loud clicking noise, finally does him more harm than good. Losing thus all the advantages of his knowledge, he now finds himself like a common or garden dunce invited to write a hundred times: I must not snap my fingers in class, in every mood, in every tense – which anyway shouldn't give him too much of a problem, seeing that he is so brilliant in every subject, and therefore in grammar – but he's equally brilliant at sport, which is unfair. Basically, though, what he's paying for are his perpetual good marks; the punishment is aimed at removing all suspicion of favouritism.

If they take care not to pick on anyone who knows, that of course is in order to pick on someone who is known, unless by an improbable chance, not to know. And the said someone knows this so well that he tries to make himself inconspicuous behind a classmate's back, keeping his head down behind the hinged top of his desk, trusting in a miraculous isochromatism that will make him merge into the wood, while the authority sends a sweeping glance across the whole class in search of a choice victim, well and truly ignorant, nice and ripe, without for a moment dreaming that this ignorance may actually be partly due to him. As his gaze is now hovering over the right-hand side of the benches where you are not sitting, you immediately feel enormously relieved, and full of compassion for the poor favoured wretch on the other side of the central

47

aisle, because after all it might just as well be him as you. Everyone his turn. But then suddenly, the outstretched arm of the authority breaks ranks with the axis of his gaze, opening an ever-widening angle to his line of vision, and his pointing index finger, seemingly autonomous, abruptly stops at you, and is shortly followed by a smile from the said authority, who turns his head in delayed action, delighted that his crude ruse has worked once again.

But it really is you, and naturally the only things you have at your disposal with which to meet the question are a mind bogged down in reflections on the extraordinary bad luck that has overwhelmed you, and a stunned silence. You even seem to realise that the other (let's call him Fraslin, because given the list of his misdeeds there's nothing scandalous in making him carry the can) is now trying to hold you up to ridicule by inciting you to reply to a totally stupid question of the order of: If man descends from the apes and the apes descend from the coconut palm, we conclude syllogistically that man descends from . . . ? Well, from what? From whatwhat-what? And the suggested response comes out the way you lay your head on the block: From the coconut palm. Bravo, triple idiot, quadruple numskull, quintuple nincompoop, a hundred thousand million lines: And I descend from the donkey, in every mood, every tense, every person, in every language, in order to show the whole world that the highest summit of stupidity culminates a few metres above sea level, at the Collège Saint-Cosmes, Saint-Nazaire, Loire-Atlantique, Brittany, France, Europe, The Earth, The Solar System, The Milky Way, The Universe.

Religious instruction, as was only right, was a serious subject in this world of cassocks . . . (Correction, though:

48

some of them, among whom was the one we called Juju, had recently abandoned the long black robe – often too short, and revealing great big clodhoppers. This robe was fitted at the waist with an abdominal belt whose apparent purpose was to act as a repository for the wearer's thumbs. In its place they had adopted a severe, dark-grey clergy-man's suit, black shirt, white stand-up collar, the last vestige of the previous uniform, with a little silver cross pinned to their lapel so that no one could mistake this costume for that of any ordinary elegant gentleman. *These* gentlemen, however, dressed in this way and hence having assumed human shape, could seriously begin to consider indulging one day in holy wedlock.)

We were hearing about the mystery of the Trinity, one of the fundamental dogmas, that's to say the rule of three (The Father, the Son and the Holy Spirit) in one (God), which had given rise to splendid exchanges in the Councils of Nicaea and Constantinople, all parties tearing each others's guts out over the consubstantiality of the Son with the Father ("engendered, not created"), a debate which Gyf settled in his own way by suddenly declaring, although no one had asked him, that it was the winning Treble. A metaphysical stupor spread over the classroom ranks. The angels who are said to pass during any pregnant pause came swishing back and forth, and collided in an ear-splitting silence. We were all expecting the ground to open up beneath us, the sky to pour down a rain of fire on the head of the blasphemer, the magisterium to cast down fulminating flame from its red-hot arm. But the kindly Juju, one eye on the floor and the other on Gyf, the kindly Juju, because he certainly had to be kind when he could so easily have crucified the speaker, contented himself with saying, in a solemn voice, that these were not joking matters, and went on to make an erudite distinction, among those who denied consubstantiality, between the Homoiousians (similar but not identical substance – which was not it itself very enlightening), and the Homoousians (non-substantial similarity – hardly more enlightening) and the Anomoeans (to sum up: the Father is the father and the Son is not the father.)

But we finally got used to Gyf's misdemeanours. We counted on him so much that we waited without budging, as mere spectators, for his reaction. Faced with a tricky situation, a flagrant injustice or a comic scene, we asked ourselves: What will Gyf do? And sometimes Gyf did nothing, remained indifferent, almost as if he were someone else, as if he suddenly seemed to have wearied of being the only one to carry the burden of rebellion on his shoulders. For instance, there were some days when he proved astonishingly studious, paying attention, putting his hand up to answer questions, when he seemed pleased to be awarded a good-conduct certificate, upset by a wrong answer which, given his efforts, it wouldn't have been charitable to mock, with the result that the authority, not wishing to discourage these newfound good intentions, took it upon himself to consider the answer practically right, which mitigated the distress of the ex-rebel. At such moments we could almost believe in the miracle of a repentant Gyf. But his conversion seemed so precarious, so fragile, that the whole class, fearing a relapse, combined to encourage him on his new path. We fell into line with him, and it was at that time that thirty exemplary pupils became interested in the fate of rosa, a rose, in the garden of Hadrian's villa.

And when the Latin teacher asked Georges-Yves (his surname was something like François, hence the abbreviation into Gyf) how it happened that there was a dative instead of an ablative, and did Georges-Yves know the name of the gulf where the famous battle between the Romans and the Venetians took place, and went on to say that Georges-Yves would certainly be able to tell us the phrase that that vindictive statesman Cato kept repeating to the senators, wouldn't he? Delenda est? Come on, Georges-Yves, delenda est? And suddenly, by way of response, we heard the sound of a cow mooing, produced by a little cylindrical metal box that you merely had to turn upside down. Georges-Yves, bring that to me at once.

IN FACT THE JOY, the tremendous explosion of joy that marked the end of the week at Saint-Cosmes, was shortlived: it lasted for as long as it took to make a dash for the door and, once at a good distance from the school, pause on the pavement facing the sea, put your bag down and get your breath back. After that, everything happened too quickly: more than an hour in the bus, with stops at the shipyards and in every village to let the workmen out, before getting home, taking it a bit easy in the evening, and then happily sleeping in your own bed. But when you woke up in the morning, all you could think of was the misery of going back. It was all over.

It was the tradition for the youth teams to play football on Sunday mornings, and in the afternoons we buttressed ourselves against the hours to stop them going by too quickly; this mainly consisted in following the kitchen clock in its fatal countdown at the same time as doing our homework, playing cards or, later, watching everything there was to be seen on television, including the interludes – a little picture puzzle of a train embedded in a filmed landscape. But even before it was time to get your things together for the following week, you were already sick at the idea of being back at school the next day. Sunday evenings are beyond rescue.

For a long time our only Sunday outing, which finally became the purpose of a walk, was devoted to visiting the paternal grave. The cemetery is some way outside the village, as they often are when the dead have been moved from the precincts of the church, so you get very used to walking, it becomes a habit by force of circumstance, now that the one and only head of the family is reposing under his granite tombstone. True, it isn't a very great distance, but at eleven you still see things from the child's point of view, and a few hundred metres seem like a hike.

So, without realising it, you become a kind of specialist in the mortuary domain. The moment anyone starts talking about death, burial, mourning, cemeteries, irreparable loss, inconsolable grief, eternal regrets, you prick up your ears: this is your department. You have your word to say. To say what? Nothing, actually, but you adopt the wise expression of someone who knows. Who knows what? That these things happen. But the result is that you move in this shadowy realm like a fish in water. Later this will make you kick yourself because, having so often played the great thanatological manitou, you are always the one called on, in painful circumstances, to write the messages of condolence. For the moment, this superior manner of pushing on open doors is the best way you have found of making it known that the things that happen, well, they've happened to you too, that's to say not directly, or you wouldn't be there to tell the tale, but to someone close to you, so close, so impossible to disentangle from yourself that you let it be understood that some part of you has also disappeared. And, although you fiercely reject the idea, that is your pathetic way of begging for pity.

Therefore, when you are asked to write an essay on a Sunday in the country, after giving it a great deal of thought, pen in mouth and eyes gazing into the middle distance, having eliminated the hoary old subjects (I do

odd jobs with Grandfather, I go fishing with Grandmother, I look for birds' nests with my cousins), you get
a kind of revelation, you decide on a sort of truth game,
the exact opposite of all those stories made up by harassed
schoolboys, and you jump at the opportunity to pull all
the stops out in a meticulous description of your visits
to the cemetery.

Everything was there. First of all the route, which starts
with the main street, which people here call the Route de
Paris, a slightly pompous appellation intended to allow us
to bask in the distant lights of the capital, and incorrect,
what's more, given the narrowness of the street (at its most
congested point, where it leaves the square, they had had
to demolish a dilapidated house on the corner to unjam the
first combine harvester, a gigantic machine for that time,
which had tried to force its way through). Since the road
loses its pavements on the outskirts of the village (not
because of any hasty decision on the part of the local
council but, like a river merging with the sands, because
the kerbs had been neglected and their concrete surface
had broken up and disappeared), all four of us marched
along the grass verges in Indian file, so as not to get run
over by the cars or caught up in the slipstream of the
lorries shooting up behind us, walking the tightrope
between the tarmac and the ditch, which wasn't very easy,
especially for Mother's high heels. Although she had
adopted widow's weeds and many signs of renunciation,
Mother could never bring herself to walk in flat-heeled
shoes, hence the non-stop, permanently-hurried jog-trot
which remains her trademark.

Once past the wide downhill bend we came to the
outer, schistose-stone wall crowned with self-propagating
plants: weeds, poppies and wallflowers. A few crosses

us an example, and he never lets himself go. Only when, hammer in hand, he hits one of his fingers very hard, does he come out with a string of stentorian invectives in which the sacred name of God is served up with all the sauces of blasphemy.

If he still intimidates us, then, it must mean that he isn't far away. Otherwise, why, whereas when we entered the cemetery we were delighted – as far as is possible in such a place, of course – to spot the famous bunch of flowers, why, when we reached his grave, did we suddenly fall silent? Because he wouldn't have appreciated it. Because he's there. And anyway, as in the game of hide-and-seek, the moment the gravel stops crunching under our feet we feel we are getting warm, we would only have to lift up the stone to discover the source of heat and bring our loved one out of hiding. But that would be too cruel. What would that make him look like, this father unmasked, trapped, enjoined to return to a life which he was probably only moderately enamoured of, since he left us to our present condition of floundering alone in a tear-filled swimming pool? So we play the game, pretending to be seeking, but not finding him. We abandon him to his sad fate of being somebody perfectly concealed from the eyes of the living.

So that people don't think us completely out of our minds, we pretend to believe that his flesh is decomposing, his bones are whitening, and that with time, by the combined action of the acidity of the soil and the infiltration of water, they will finally return to dust. Because that is the official version, which it's always wise to conform to. But when, standing there at the edge of the grave as if on the edge of an abyss, silent, contemplative, our hands joined over our pelvic area, with lowered heads and moist eyes, we mumble "Our Father who art in Heaven", as if the prayer had been written especially for him, we feel in our guts that nothing happens the way they say it does: that's to say, that business of decomposition. And none of their eyewitness accounts, none of their exhumations, can do anything about it. In our innermost depths, in this silent sanctum into which none but the faintest echoes of life penetrate, in this place which refuses to accept the obvious or to cast out the nines, in which strange thoughts drift around, in this heart of hearts from which a torrent of confused words are addressed to the man lying in ambush, everything happens as if, on the contrary, his glorious body were still intact.

This image of his body isn't a precise reflection of the mortal coil from whose broad outlines it takes its inspiration, no doubt in order to facilitate its identification, it doesn't tell you anything about a particular wrinkle round his eyelids or at the corner of his lips, it won't tell you what colour his eyes were if you happen to have forgotten, it won't prevent the erosion of his features in your memory. But, however imperfect it may be in depicting him in detail (although on the whole faithful to the spirit of the man who has gone, to our idea of him), it nevertheless has this advantage over the other one, the flesh and blood one, in that it is far more resistant to the outrages of time. It hasn't even anything to fear from any confusion of memory. The reason? Moulded in the void left by our absent father, this glorious body very precisely represents the figure of loss.

Sometimes, at his graveside, the feeling of his presence is so strong, the idea of his dissolution so absurd, that you surprise yourself by raising your eyes up to heaven, to the skies where, in your imagination, the compassionate, reassuring, totally tranquil face of your vanished father is inscribed. And it is so crystal clear, this impression of that radiant tranquillity welcoming you through the looking glass of appearances, that you envy it to the point of raising your head and searching for traces of it among the clouds. But in the twinkling of an eye the visible world resumes its rights: up there you find no face, no hint of a smile, not even one of those blue patches with which our region is miserly but which, even if it wouldn't console you, would at least have allowed you to avoid feeling overwhelmed. Just clouds, masses of clouds, dark and low, clouds billowing over or stretching out like dirty cotton wool from west to east, heavy with oceanic fluids, advancing in waves on various levels, at different speeds, so that they seem to be engaged in a crazy race above the earth, as if they had no wish to linger there, their upper and lower strata sometimes dissociating themselves from one another in their choice of direction, some opting for orthodromy, others for a more northerly route, the indefatigable activity of fugitives, the savage hordes of the Atlantic setting out to conquer the world, and their disarray is such that wisps of haze become detached from the lowest layers, like the weak elements, thrown on one side, of a moving flock, the tatters of a dead firmament which droop like the sails of a ghost ship, float in the wind, cling to the tops of the trees, and subside into the distance.

Realising that there is nothing to be expected from those skies, apart from wind, clouds and rain, you lower your head sadly, and shut your eyes. But you have hardly had time to brood over your disappointment when once again, inscribed behind your eyelids against an azure background, you see that radiant face. And this earth-sky return trip concluded my account of a Sunday in the country.

WELL, YOU KNOW WHAT? this essay? what good it did me? To start with, let's think back to the cruel ceremony of homework being given back: the master stands in the middle of the classroom handing everyone, or having it passed to him, his marked composition, and accompanies this rite with comments which obviously have to be sarcastic (since only silence is equivalent to praise), and which are designed to be greeted by mocking laughter from the whole class, a sort of obsequious bleating sound in which the lucky recipient does his best to join, however bitter his disappointment, thus demonstrating that he can be a good loser and also laugh at himself.

To save his best effects until the last, and, according to whether his fancy opted either for keeping the good pupils in suspense and sowing doubt in their minds, or on the contrary for treating himself to a bit of fun at the expense of the time-honoured dunce as the grande finale, he would start sometimes with the worst marks, sometimes with the best. The boy who regularly languished at the bottom of the class, the one who greeted with a quietly ironic smile the most pessimistic remarks about his future based on the pretext that such a lamentable result didn't open up any very encouraging prospects, Gyf, was no longer there. He had left us at the end of the first year, expelled no doubt, his indiscretions having finally prevailed over the extenuating circumstances he enjoyed on account of his family situation. At the start of the next school year we had noticed his absence with dismay; we foresaw a joyless year to come. Which indeed it was, because it was on our return from the Christmas holiday a few months later that my schoolmates saw me for the first time in my condition of a fatherless orphan.

My evocation of a Sunday in the country spoke of nothing else. I was eagerly awaiting the result, sure at least that with this account of a visit to the cemetery I wasn't duplicating the inevitable fishing trips, the tall tales that were useful in such cases as no one ever demanded the slightest proof: for instance, why didn't they ever ask for the produce of this miraculous fishing expedition to be tucked between the pages of the essay – the thirty-kilo carp or the hundreds of little roaches? Personally, I had nothing to fear, they could even send an investigator to the spot, everything was there, exactly as I had described it, although with the possible exception of the gilded, lanceolate spikes on the wrought-iron gate – your memory sometimes superimposes previous memories, borrows from here or there, from the gate of a prefecture, for instance, but for the essential, at least, I ran no risk of being caught out, and then, how could any teacher marking an essay want, by a vicious verdict, to take the responsibility for piling misery upon misery?

The essays succeeded one another, the marks decreased and the number of candidates for the bottom place was reduced. Soon, the man standing in the middle of the classroom was holding up the last essay and brandishing it as if to say you haven't seen anything yet, meaning something like the be-all and end-all, the last straw, the sort of thing you have to see to believe – and I was now the only one who hadn't been served. The sentence was about to be pronounced, and it was going to be accompanied by the most terrible insults. That page flapping about as if caught in the gusts of a violent storm was going to come crashing down in a torrent of abuse.

He announced that this last place was a great first: what would you say to being bottom of the class? That's never happened to you before, has it? You protest feebly, trying to show by nodding your head that you *have* already been in such a situation. Which isn't true. It's even completely unusual. Simply, by your denial, by your trivialisation of what was supposed to be unheard of, you are hoping to attenuate the violence of his remarks, to moderate the histrionic effect of the flailing sleeves of the pitiless prosecutor. Pathetic display, pathetic respite. As if he didn't have the right to the last word. And don't you think it's unfair that only the best pupils are invited to mount the podium? An essay like this, however – the page he's holding up in the air flaps even more wildly – is a kind of exploit. Well then, get up on the table and crow like a cock. And he takes you by the hand, hoists you up on to the bench and ceremoniously hands you your essay, peppered with comments in red ink both in the margins and between the lines, with words crossed out or corrected, like blood flowing on the back of an animal pierced by banderillas, and you haven't the slightest idea what you can have done to deserve such ferocity, you are choking back the inexorable upsurge of tears with the greatest difficulty, and while from your perch you can see through the window the sea churning down below, smashing into the breakwaters, spreading its sheets of foam over the pebble beach and marking the limit of its advance with a frieze of brown wrack, you feel that your internment is total, that even the ocean is hostile to you because in one fraternal act it could easily submerge Saint-Cosmes, it could extract one mighty breaker from that useless liquid mass and put an abrupt end to your calvary, you feel, with amazement, that the world, as if it had nothing better to do, is taking cowardly advantage of the departure of the great absentee to league all its forces against you, you feel, finally, that you are alone, helpless.

Was it in anticipation of all these future ordeals? I had received the gift of tears at a very early age. Strictly speaking, though, this gift isn't much of a present. What does it make you look like when you're forever snivelling over the slightest little thing, an unkind remark or a thoughtful gesture, always a tear keeping watch at the corner of your eye, ready to be shed at the slightest emotion? It makes you wonder where on earth they can tuck themselves away, these salt-water swimming pools that swell your eyelids after they have already overflowed, when anyone would be inclined to imagine the opposite: dropsical eyelids that could be emptied by a tearful session, but the worst thing is that these reactive tears don't always flow deliberately. There's nothing more uncontrollable: your heart doesn't seem affected, at least it doesn't appear to be on fire, and yet the fire-engine hoses automatically switch themselves on. In spite of yourself. And there's absolutely no way you can hold these tears back. Or perhaps just for a moment, if you keep your eyes obstinately open, if you stare at the ocean and curse it for remaining deaf to your calvary. But you know from experience that this film somehow or other clinging to your pupil as duckweed on a pond will collapse without warning and set off a deluge you won't be able to control, thus making you even more vulnerable, and that this obvious sign of your suscepti- bility will immediately classify you among the weaklings –

a high-risk classification in the world of school. Because before they start marvelling at your sensitivity, before the inevitable malcontent is metamorphosed into a monster of compassion – and the truth, of course, is elsewhere – for a long time you will have had to endure the sarcasm of the self-styled tough guys who see no difference between having a hard heart and keeping their feelings under control, and who, if they ran out of grief, would not for anything in the world allow themselves to have a transfusion.

In this domain, however, my reputation was well established. Just one example from the previous year, when this was not yet a matter of life and death, because none of the members of the household was then missing.

We were given our letters at lunchtime, usually when we were having our dessert, and as they were always opened it was wise to warn our correspondents beforehand, for while *they* ran no risk, if they used any sort of bad language they could put us in a delicate situation. As for the letters we sent, naturally they were dissected, analysed, and possibly commented on to the writer if by any chance, while recognising the extraordinary quality of the food, he had allowed some reservations to appear between the lines on the succulence of, let's say, noodle omelettes. Summoned to the headmaster's study, the latter, with the said letter in his hand, would read the culprit the incriminating passage, and require him to explain at length his pretensions to the role of gastronomic critic, which could well have harmful consequences to the reputation of Saint-Cosmes, the very acme of good living, as was proved by its incomparable situation along the seashore. Everyone envies us, but Monsieur turns up his nose, would Monsieur have any objection to copying out the recipe for noodle omelette three thousand times, and then starting again since he will have left out the salt? Gyf (because every Monday evening we had to send our weekly report home), as he didn't really have anyone to write to, took this roundabout way of recording a kind of indirect list of grievances for the attention of the authorities. In this manner, he had written in one of his letters that the hardest part wasn't the long sessions on his knees imposed on him by the dormitory supervisor, but the fact that the said supervisor, with whom he shared the intimate hours of his penitence, was reluctant for long days on end to change his socks. Which was notorious. Whether by chance or as a result of a remonstrance from the authorities, the owner of the hypersensitive arches of the foot did after that make an effort.

And yet the letter didn't contain any very terrible news. Aunt Marie, our old Aunt Marie, who had been abruptly dismissed from the convent school where she had taught for fifty years, after which she had been moping in her little house for a few months, had just had a fall and broken her arm. A broken arm isn't the end of the world: they put it in plaster, then all her friends sign their names on it, and forty days later, that's it. Although you couldn't be too sure about the signatures, as the old retired schoolmistress was probably past the age for that, but once the fracture had mended she would soon be able to resume her writings, which mainly consisted of copying out prayers in the hope of increasing the yield of her already considerable capital of days of indulgence. So there was nothing cataclysmic about the news, which apparently wasn't even the main reason for the letter that the kindly Juju was holding out to me, at the same time specifying that it didn't contain anything serious. He himself had had a similar accident a few years before, and he had got over it very well. What's more, to back his statement up with a demonstration, he began jerking his arm up and down as if he was operating the village pump. Which only goes to show that opening other people's correspondence is a delicate exercise which in certain circumstances calls for an infinite amount of tact.

And yet, even when thus prepared, there is nothing you can do to stem the Tethys of tears always lying in wait behind your eyelids to seize on the slightest pretext to overflow. My fromage blanc was soon drowned, the dessert that my seven table companions were sadly coveting; they had got into the habit of sharing my rations, so when it came to seating arrangements, I was one of the most in demand.

During my first year at school, repelled by food that was nothing like my mother's home cooking, I had got into the habit of taking my basic nourishment in the form of slices of bread and butter, and sugar lumps: twelve and a half in my morning bowl of the white coffee which was brought to us – already sugared – in big aluminium pots, on trolleys with cream-coloured tubular frames, by two scraggy, mustachioed old nuns entrammelled in thick black dresses protected in front by white aprons under which hung a rosary. The little sisters' skin was flaking under their coifs, it was so long since they had gone about bareheaded. They had taken such strict vows of penitence that their scalps had necessarily suffered. Although *we* had been told often enough that a good airing was a hygienic measure. The moment he entered the classroom the Authority hastened to open the windows, saying loudly: It smells of wild animals in here. (After which the same wild animals got called worms, slugs or drones, according to the inspiration of the moment, although it had much more to do with the opinion the same Authority had formed of his menagerie.) The animal life under the coifs was no doubt more closely related to the microbic domain, but the little sisters' foreheads, irritated by the starched white linen which gave a Boris Karloff look to the tops of their heads, presented worrying signs of alopecia and, as bits of unidentified skin floated on the surface of our white coffee, we always wondered if they actually were lacteal. The twelve and a half sugar lumps were a necessity.

Thanks to which – to this kind of exploit, which after all was pretty unusual – I had rapidly become famous. The full complement of Saint-Cosmes marched past incredulously at breakfast time (when, having been up at a quarter past six, we had already endured an hour of study and a stint in the chapel where, still half asleep, we mumbled our way through a kind of Lauds), to count the twelve and a half lumps with me. Incredible, inconceivable, undrinkable, I was mortgaging my life, my organism, my pancreas. They talked in veiled terms about dental suicide (and it did in fact cost me two molars, blackened up to the gum – you see, my dear little girl, sugar is very bad for the teeth, but do have another sweet if you really want one). Even Gyf trotted out his party piece: my white coffee was so saturated that half the sugar lumps didn't even melt. And indeed I did find half of them, apparently intact, at the bottom of my bowl, but, like the objects on the *Titanic*, the moment you remove them from the liquid element they fall to bits. So I used to scrape up the remains of my syrup with a teaspoon. But basically, what most intrigued the mob of doubting Thomases was that half lump, the result of long and patient experimentation fraught with untoward trials and changes of mind. So, holding back my tears, I had to explain that thirteen were too many, but that with only twelve it was still a bit bland.

Thanks to which, again – to this butter and sugar diet – I only grew four centimetres in the first year, while my friends, accumulating a lack of taste with noodle omelettes and compotes of tinned apples, grew a head and shoulders taller in the same period. It must also be said that they had the advantage of an extra portion, mine, which, with my permission, they either appropriated, shared, or tossed up for. And this was why Gyf, thinking ahead, afraid that this deluge of tears would engulf our fromage blanc, surreptitiously shifted my plate sideways and, as he started digging his spoon into it, took – may I? – the letter from my hands, determined to discover the source of the tragedy that was causing us such great distress. At the very least it would have to be that my entire family had been exterminated. A version that hardly tallied with the kindly Juju's remarks which – unless you took the symbolism of his pumping arm to mean something like: It's all the same to me, which was not at all his style – were certainly intended to be reassuring.

When he had taken in the contents of the letter, Gyf reported on them to the petrified onlookers round the table and explained that there was really no cause for alarm, in other words nothing to break your heart over, just a question of an old aunt having broken her arm, and as he gulped down my fromage blanc, that the only thing that explained my behaviour was my propensity (I'm translating) for snivelling. Whereupon his attention was drawn to the fact that no one had heard me, between snivels, officially give him my dessert, and that he therefore ought to share it out equitably. Maybe, but he was the one who had read the letter, and that gave him rights. Rights my foot, replied a bush lawyer, proceeding forthwith to a distraint of the plate, while I was preparing my defence: of course a broken arm was nothing much, but you mustn't forget the victim's age, seventy-two, and then don't forget either that great oaks from little acorns grow and hence great misfortunes from little worries, which meant that they had better just wait and see. And so had I, at that.

Events were in fact to prove me right, but for the moment Gyf, not caring to be outmanoeuvred, made another violent grab at the plate and finally got hold of it when the other jouster let go of it, but minus the fromage blanc which, taking advantage of this catapult effect, ended up partly splashed over his glasses, and partly over the smart clergyman's suit of our kindly (although somewhat less so in the circumstances) Juju, who had come to the rescue to separate the two starvelings. Whereupon, since our reward was to be deprived of dessert for several days, everyone agreed that it was all my fault. The life of a weeping willow is not a bed of roses.

And now, standing on my bench, I should surely have had a right to let myself go. Misfortunes, of which my aunt's broken arm had been the fateful omen, had descended on us in deluge after deluge. For the death of our father had been followed, three months later, by that of Aunt Marie, struck dead by a broken heart, and for the first time in her life reproaching Heaven, although she had always as a good Christian accepted the trials it sent her, trusting in a mysterious but benevolent divine concern for her, and hence believing that it was all right for two of her brothers to have been killed in the war, for the third not to have survived the death of his wife, leaving their nineteen-year-old son to her vigilant affection, for her young sister to have been carried off by the Spanish influenza, for herself to have had for all consolation, apart from religion and her two nephews, nothing but the schoolmistress's transmission of her body of knowledge to three generations of little girls, and that it was still all right for her to lead the life of a semi-recluse between her little house and the convent school (just a very small sacrifice in comparison with the infinite bliss in Heaven that she had a right to expect), but the sudden death at the age of forty-one of her beloved nephew – this time it was *not* all right, it was unforgivable. It was as if her spirit had been pushed over the yellow line of the intolerable, beyond which doubt began to instil its terrible poison. And so it was an Aunt Marie who was within a hair's-breadth of renunciation who sank – wherein we should perhaps see the hand of Providence aiming to save our Aunt Marie the Blessed, before her faltering reason could lead her into blasphemy – into a long coma that lasted several weeks and reached its conclusion one nineteenth of March, Saint Joseph's day, the day of the eponymous patron saint of her brother and her nephew.

Notified by a telephone call, the kindly Juju summoned me to the playground and, with a solemn air, one eye on me and the other straining to distinguish a tridactyl seagull from a herring gull, gave me the bad news: Your aunt is dead. And then, after a pause for thought, while Tethys was welling up under my eyelids, fearing a possible misunderstanding: You know which one? Of course I knew. Aunt Mathilde, Aunt Lucie, Aunt Marthe all being in good health, it was more logical for death to have chosen the comatose old schoolmistress. Whereupon, relieved, he suggested that I should withdraw to the study room, pack my things and take the bus for Random that evening, never imagining that a few weeks' later he would have to summon me once more, this time into his own study whose double doors, the second one padded, protected him from indiscretions and allowed him to raise his voice.

The repetition became almost comic, which didn't help matters. To have to repeat almost word for word the same macabre avowal removed some of the solemnity from his announcement. So he made short work of telling me that my grandfather had just died. You know which one? His roving eye was desperately trying to fasten on to the curtains, while he was reproaching himself for having allowed himself to be carried away by his own momentum, for not having watched his tongue. He could hear himself echoing the same remarks after only a few weeks. For two pins he would have asked to be pitied. Yes, but – of the two, surely the more to be pitied was the one who had been repeatedly plunged into mourning in his twelfth year?

As for the other grandfather, it was a long time since he had been out of the running, as he had died of grief when Aline, his beloved wife, succumbed to a Rimbaldian symptom, a problem with her knee, but the kindly Juju was no longer listening. He was silently congratulating himself that the boy's father had chosen to pass on during the Christmas holidays, and so spared him a painful chore. But he needn't have worried. There would have been no possible doubt there, either.

As I was getting down from my bench, lowering my head to hide my rising tears, my glasses, no doubt dragged down by the weight of the thick, heavy lenses, fell off. This had already happened many times, and the unbreakable lenses (at least they were sold as such) – which in fact made life very much more pleasant for the myopic – had so far proved shock-proof. They had one drawback, though: while they didn't break, they did easily become scratched. So you went around with a kind of spider's web – the scratches – floating in front of your eyes, which for a long time you vainly tried to dispel by blinking, or by endlessly wiping your glasses with a handkerchief, or, if you were the cautious type who kept your original spectacle case in spite of having no further use for it since you have been told you must wear your glasses all the time, with the sort of little yellow duster with the name and address of the optician emblazoned on it together with a picture of a pair of pince-nez, which was the only present you got from your myopia.

But unbreakable – not really, only in comparison with traditional lenses. Let's rather say more resistant, but within limits, and so one of the lenses – which were only attached to the frame by a bit of nylon thread running round the rims – came out, fell on the tiled floor and smashed into smithereens, sending little crystals flying in all directions under the desks.

Every unforeseen event was usually more than welcome. During the time it took for the autocrat on duty to get things back in hand, we allowed ourselves a certain amount of dissipation. Those closest to the drama took advantage of it, then, to play games of the order of: the classroom has been flooded (or invaded by cockroaches), lifting their feet off the floor, picking up their schoolbags which had been resting against the foot of their desks, and refusing to take an interest in the lesson so long as they were living under the menace of this glass peril. The terrible Fraslin, who had for a moment believed he could carry on by ignoring the incident (this intention being not so much benevolent as cruel – what could I do, half blinded as I was, without being given permission to react?), pretended to be wondering who was responsible for this shambles (as if it was on my own initiative that I had climbed up on to the bench), and, after putting up a show of acting fairly, sent me off to find a broom in the cupboard of the classroom next door. This wasn't exactly much of a pleasure either: having to face an equally malevolent teacher, his demands for an explanation, his sarcastic remarks, his calling his class to witness, and finally his sempiternal and depressing: Don't forget to bring it back (as if I might be irresistibly tempted to make off with his precious broom).

With which I went back to my classroom sheepishly – just look at you, put it down in a corner, sit down and look at the ceiling, you can sweep up during break – and I realised at once that the despot had taken advantage of my absence to start on a new exercise, which meant, in so far as I had missed the beginning and it was impossible to copy from a classmate, that I was in for a future zero with its accompanying punishment. Which goes to show that ruthlessness is an art.

Even when I was back in my place, my troubles were far from over: raising my eyes, I clearly perceived that without glasses I couldn't see very much. If the Authority told me to look at the ceiling, that was because it didn't present any great interest in itself, so it was no handicap if it had lost some of its clarity, but what was more worrying was that the greenboard, seen from my bench, was now covered in indecipherable whitish marks, as if the chalk cloud raised by the wiper was never going to settle, was invading space and becoming even denser in the distance. And, with my tears mixing in, everything became a blur, forming a foggy mud in front of my eyes which accentuated my isolation, kept the world at a distance, and reinforced my retreat into myself.

I picked up my glasses, or what remained of them, deplored the cost of the disaster (unbreakable lenses were naturally more expensive and we couldn't count on a reimbursement from the Social Security, or if we could it would be so negligible that it would really be making a mockery of us – a recurrent theme in a family of modest means who all wore glasses and who weren't far from considering this ostracism of precariously-sighted people to be a form of immanent injustice, added to the fact that in any case shopkeepers, another leitmotif, never have any rights to anything, unlike civil servants who get free travel, grants for their children, and only work when they feel like it), and put them back on my nose. In front of my right eye the nylon thread had become contorted into a figure of eight. My left eye could see a good deal better because, as the frames had been warped in their fall, the intact lens was lying flat in my eye-socket like a monocle – which, the year before, had been Gyf's trademark.

When I closed my eyes one after the other, then, I had

a choice between two visions, between two worlds. The first, perfectly clear, in which certain things stood out: the mocking smile of the Authority, a grammatical rule on the board, the colour of the beaks and feet of the tridactyl seagulls (which is how you distinguish them from herring gulls), the contour of the leaves on the trees in the playground (which is how you recognise the lime trees), a whole world so sure of itself that it even makes an exhibition of itself, and the other one, considerably shrunken (the horizon reduced to three metres), imprecise and vague, a eulogy to the soft-focus effect, in which the sky could be taken for an upside-down sea and the clouds for seething foam, in which the green blackboard has nothing to reveal but its chalk veil, in which faces are faceless and therefore without malice, and life is padded, muffled, has lost its definition, and seems to have become the antechamber to another world.

With the further consequence that the elementary laws of physics thereby become modified. For instance, sound, in the world of the myope, travels faster than light. It's by a voice, not by a look, that you realise that someone is talking to you. It's the sound of an engine, rather than the last-minute appearance of a car, that stops you crossing a road. Provocative looks leave you stony cold, an affectionate word moves you to tears. Wrinkles become attenuated, and as the tone of a voice preserves its grain of youth for a long time, you get the idea that the people around you are not as susceptible to ageing as is generally thought.

No one needs to be persuaded of the advantages of good, clear eyesight. It stops you saying hallo to lamp-posts, or sitting on your glasses, or pushing open the door to the kitchen instead of to the lavatory in restaurants, or looking for hours for a needle in a haystack because you thought it was a bundle of wheat, but within the perimeter of the attenuated life (attenuated, like sounds in the fog) in which I had been living since that fatal day after Christmas, in the centre of my nebula, in the haze of death that envelops the survivors, you don't expect clarity to provide all the light.

You don't expect very much, actually, but you hope not so much for commiseration as for a little consideration. For it's a severe blow, after all, and it would be charitable not to make it any worse. Well then, with the spectacles of the one-eyed on my nose, with my essay in my hand, I couldn't believe my eyes. My torturer hadn't been satisfied with scribbling savagely all over my pages in red ink and with giving me bottom marks, he had also raised objections in a few lines of caustic comments, firstly to my unpolished, irresolute style (has anyone ever seen a cross sway? With which I certainly agreed; of course a cross doesn't sway, even in a strong wind, but when we were always having it dinned into us that we must vary our vocabulary and use verbs expressing movement instead of auxiliary verbs, we got to the point, terrorised and against our will, of committing such aberrations), and his next objection was that I hadn't really dealt with the subject (in case you've forgotten: describe a Sunday in the country).

What was he trying to insinuate? That Random was not a rural commune? To transform us into town-dwellers was pretty flattering, but why in that case did the same Authority not hesitate to accuse me, and some of the other boarders like me, of being peasants? A rapid review of the scene soon set the record straight: any expert who had noticed the absence of gilded, lanceolate spikes on the entrance gate of the cemetery couldn't deny the rustic character, with its herds of cows ambling down the main street, with its tractors, and even its horse-drawn carts, of this little commune in the Loire-Atlantique. As for Sundays, leisure activities were so rare that you would have been hard put to find anything else to do: go dancing? too young. A game of football? We played in the mornings. Fishing? Random isn't on the banks of the Loire, and anyway that wasn't at all our style (nor, among other things, was picnicking; can you imagine our delicate young widow eating a joint of chicken in her fingers?). Blackberry picking? And why not whale hunting? On Sundays – and here we are by no means straying from the subject, but in its very heart – we visited our father under his granite tombstone.

It was very precisely since that monumental landmark of the day after Christmas, when an arterial abnormality (or over-indulgence in cigarettes, or an impossibly exhausting job, or unfitness for life, or the example of his parents who themselves died too soon, or an ancient feeling of guilt at being the sole survivor among his still-born brothers and sisters) took him from the affection of his family and friends (the commutative formula). To which, before the cemetery ritual is organised, three days must be added.

Count them: death during the night of Thursday to Friday, the time taken by the administrative and religious formalities – no funeral ceremonies are conducted on Sundays – therefore, wait for Monday. Which is a long time for a corpse. Not that it can't stay motionless, but the nauseating, sugary smell that gradually envelops it began to be a little troublesome, while, on hearing the unbelievable news, people we knew and people we didn't know came in flocks to embrace the grief-stricken young widow, her eyes reddened with tears and with keeping vigil, and then remained in meditative silence for a long moment by the side of their fickle friend.

For this purpose, chairs had been requisitioned from all over the house and arranged on the three sides of the bed in anticipation of this little existential drama. Continuous performance for three days and four nights, lit in the old-fashioned way by a candle on each of the two bedside tables, the melting wax piled up in pearly droplets on the base of the candlesticks. Because nothing much has changed in the face of death: the same flame since the night of time, the same flickering light opposing the invasion of the shadows, but the patches of darkness created in this way on either side of the bloodless mask, animated by the lunar reflection of the candles, were an encouragement to silent meditation.

During the day, the solid-wood interior shutters remain closed, just allowing the infiltration of a vertical strip of grey light, whose variations in intensity inform us about the progress of the afternoon. Nothing can match the penumbra when it comes to imposing silence with natural authority. As a result, the slightest sound is invested with importance: from time to time a car or moped passing by, feet scraping the floor, the faint bump of a chair being cautiously moved, the rustle of a fabric – legs being crossed and uncrossed – the murmur of a prayer. Another virtue of the dark is that you don't have to adopt the appropriate expression, which is practically obligatory in daylight. Some faces which don't reveal any sign of their emotions might well be reproached for insensitivity. Whereas the veil of the shadow projected on to the walls covers everyone's thoughts in a shower of ashes.

Because people interpret everything, you know, and never so much as in moments like these, when they pick up the slightest sign. An automatic gesture, a conventional word, become charged with an intensity which they simply do not possess. Every remark is taken literally, its every possible meaning studied and dissected. The person who has said it, however tactless it may be – you can't imagine that he doesn't mean a word of it. It's terrible –

yes, it's terrible. It's always the best who are the first to go – yes, he was the best. He's unforgettable, this man – of course we shall never forget him. A hand grasps your shoulder, and it's consolation itself that has alighted on your shoulder; a look through blurred tears, and that's the essence of grief; a benevolent smile – is this person not perhaps less affected than he makes out, when in the presence of our misery he can still find the strength to smile? We need to be handled with kid gloves. We repeat the slightest piece of information to ourselves: Your father, we used to call him the white wolf, he was so well known to us all. But surely a white wolf can only be seen as a sign of rarity, it isn't like the white rabbit, which sends you back to little girls' reveries. A wolf, that's to say a respected force, a fiercely independent spirit. And suddenly your memories of this man no longer know any frontiers, alight wherever they wish, prowl around everywhere as if on familiar ground. As if he had spent his life choosing locations where he could signpost the way ahead for us.

The time people spend in keeping vigil is variable; everyone estimates it more or less according to the measure of his grief, but there does exist a conventional minimum, which should be no less than a quarter of an hour. Below that would be to treat the dead man and his family with disrespect and risk setting tongues wagging. Above that, the plot of this tragic impromptu is too tenuous to hold for very long the attention of those who are less concerned. Taking advantage of the penumbra and a soothing silence, reverie takes flight far away from the thought of the dead man.

As an example: the young widow whom you have just clasped in your arms and who is preparing to pass through a long tunnel whose end she is afraid she will never see, a few years later, and to our great astonishment (and here we got a glimpse of a little light close to its exit), came back from one of these wakes in gales of uncontrollable laughter. Despite appearances, there was nothing scandalous about her reaction. We were within the bounds of the conceivable: a man who had died at a relatively advanced age, who had lived life to the full and had even taken great pleasure in doing so, with the result that for many years now he had been boasting that he weighed at least a hundred and twenty kilos, scales not being capable of imagining anything beyond that. No point, in such conditions, in demanding that heaven should justify itself. So this enormous man was resting in the dusk on his made-to-measure bed, his folded hands tied together to stop them slipping off that mountain of flesh. The young widow, now a little less young, noticed a resemblance that escaped her for the moment: that gross paunch, that quadruple chin swollen by the tight knot of his tie, that little moustache just a couple of fingers wide, that strand of hair plastered down over his forehead, that round head. And at the same time as she was praying for the salvation of the deceased: O Lord, welcome into your celestial abode the soul of your humble servant who always benefited from the good things you have created, she mentally added a postcript: And may I take this opportunity of asking you whether you haven't among your flock a lamb who bears a slight resemblance to this one? Oliver Hardy (of Laurel and Hardy), whispered the Lord, who has sharp eyes. That was the end. Oliver Hardy on his death bed, you expect him first to tweak his moustache convulsively, then to sneeze, and then to come up with one last gag, and anyway, Oliver Hardy is immortal. So there's no longer any reason to keep a straight face. Hence the outburst of laughter on leaving this silent film – and this good news: our mother is at the end of her long tunnel.

But in our father's case, it would have been unthinkable for us to laugh once we were out of the house. How could anyone doubt the sincerity of all those grief-stricken people filing non-stop in front of his body? Certainly there had been dead people before him, but it seemed obvious that the gap they left behind them had not been anything like so great, that the awe was not comparable, nor was the feeling of rebellion. The proof of this is that huge crowd in the bedroom, those haggard looks, those faces we are incapable of putting a name to now that they have started coming from farther and farther away, from a long way outside the commune, and even from outside the department, as the unbelievable news spread. For no other reason than to be there. And when it seems that they've been there long enough, and that the young widow has actually noticed their presence, they take advantage of a new arrival and discreetly give up their place to him.

Only the women bring rosaries. The men either don't dare, or don't believe in the power of prayer. Long ago they acquired the habit of not complaining, of not asking for anything, of simply relying on their own strength. When they do furtively make the sign of the cross, it's with the minimal movement of their arms, with their heads lowered to reduce the distance between forehead and navel, so the foot of the cross is level with the solar plexus and the extremities of its arms reach no farther than the hollows on either side of the collar bones. What you expect from the men is more like consoling words, the sort that, without drawing a line under what has just happened, reorientate you towards the future which, from the prophetic point of view, is generally situated a long way ahead, so they don't run much risk of being contradicted on the instant.

The stock phrases keep coming, old-fashioned and clumsy, embarrassed and benevolent. Like this one, to the orphans: You will reap what he has sown, repeated several times as if to hammer it home, and in such an earnest manner, with such certainty, that you begin to wonder what on earth he can have sown, this father, what philosopher's seed, what signpost to hidden treasure, which would turn the future moment when we were to reap the harvest into a sort of Easter morning, when you run out into the garden searching for the little sugared images of the Child Jesus and the chocolate eggs hidden among the laurel and the flowers.

III

An impression of déjà vu, but only fleeting, and also his hair was long, now, it hung down over his shoulders, was divided over the top of his head by a white parting and tucked back under his ears, from which he was certainly asking a lot, seeing that they also supported the sidepieces of his glasses. And that was precisely what ought to have put me on the track: the cheapest glasses, reimbursed in full, which no optician ever displayed in his shop window unless perhaps at carnival time, and which you only came across in the very back backwoods or in the destitution of an orphanage. Normally, students who didn't want to look like their parents opted for the Chekhov or Trotsky model, and the little intellectual, Spartan touch those round, metal-rimmed spectacles give. But *these* went beyond the bounds of contention. Anyone who sported such frames was most certainly not the type to accept any sort of class compromise. No doubt about it, that basic model was to be interpreted as an expression of unfailing support for the mass of our comrade workers, a fundamental claim that could only lead to a radiant future.

On the subject of the imminence of a tomorrow that would be far brighter than yesterday, it was wiser to appear optimistic, or to manage to persuade yourself that that was what you were, because it was a serious subject which probably couldn't stand up to the instillation of the poison of doubt. And in this case you could even show a certain inflexibility of character. So the stinking hyena of profit, for example, nourished in its perfidious bosom not only high finance but also small shopkeepers. What? Mother, a stinking hyena? I preferred not to pursue this point, and spoke rather of a dead father – the victim of the forces of capitalist oppression? – there was a hint of that but I didn't go into detail, although it was in a way true that he had killed himself with overwork, but it was still too soon for me to discuss and illustrate my family. All the more so in that families were not in the odour of sanctity either, and as for sanctity – let's not talk about it, so in this case let's talk about something else. But there again, the dialectical art of my brothers in arms had led me, during an ill-advised discussion on revisionism and letting land lie fallow, to conclude my argument by completely contra-dicting what I had said at the beginning, which was already not all that clear, but you have to start somehow. With the result that, faced with the mocking remarks of my objec-tors, I got myself even further bogged down by explaining that this contradiction was precisely what I had been trying to demonstrate, at the same time swearing to myself that they would never catch me doing that again. But they did, naturally, because it's hard to stay forever on the side-lines, and brothers in arms, which is one way of putting it, are totally disarmed and, all in all, pretty much alone.

And it was rare, actually, for anyone to knock on my door at the hall of residence. Its four floors without a lift weren't the only reason. I did probably make something of an effort, through an excess of caution, to discourage volunteers. So the student with the fully-reimbursed orphan's glasses wasn't the first to try his luck. A short time before, I had been visited by a fellow alumnus of Saint-Cosmes, whom I had immediately suspected of coming simply to taunt me and spy on me. Because after all, why would he have crossed the whole town, seeing that the faculty of medicine was on the opposite side to the arts faculty? To enquire after my health? to find out whether I skipped classes? to swap memories of school? All right, we had been at school together for a year or two – even though he had left us at the end of the second year – but not in the same conditions. He had been a day boy; in other words, compared with our fate he was one of the lucky ones. What's more, he came from an upper-class Saint-Nazaire family, his father was the boss of the ship-yards, or something of the sort, his mother did charity work in the parish, and it was because of their affluence and charitable duty that I had been invited one Thursday, which in those days was our day off school, to their beau-tiful house on the seafront, the sort of villa built between the wars which made you wonder how on earth it could have escaped the all-out blitz on the port and town which had turned Saint-Nazaire into a bomb site.

This invitation was all the more surprising in that I had never had the feeling that he and I were friends, or even vague allies. There were two clearly distinct groups at the school, and he wasn't one of my chain-gang compan-ions. But at least the sudden interest he showed in me enabled me to avoid the sempiternal Thursday afternoon walks, lined up in twos (fortunately we weren't required to hold hands), along the seafront, either towards the customs house or, in the opposite direction, towards the port where, in bad weather, we amused ourselves by pushing the enormous cargo boats away from the quay by giving them a simple shove with our feet. When, after walking five kilometres, we finally arrived at the chosen beach (at the foot of a cliff, a fine sandy cove enclosed by the sea when the tide was rising), we were naturally forbidden to venture into the rocks or even to dip so much as half a foot in the water, so our main concern was to organise long-jump competitions on the sand, or boring games of noughts and crosses (once you knew the trick, the game was over before it had even begun: the first to move his light-coloured shell or his dark little pebble on the grid had already won). Naturally we took a football, a clapped-out rubber ball, cratered like the surface of the moon but impossible to dribble in the fine sand, and hand-to-hand combat was even more savage. Hence the advantage of inheriting the job of goalkeeper, for which there were more candidates than usual because of the spectacular dives the playing ground made possible. Although you had to watch out for buried pebbles, rocks, dead branches, bits of broken bottles, rusty wires, which sometimes made your landing painful. At all events, given the distance and knowing that we had to be back in time for the five o'clock study period, we had no sooner arrived than, after a short sit-in, we already had to be thinking of leaving.

With the approach of summer, as our tongues were hanging out on the walk back, we were for once allowed to stop at the ice-cream stall on the edge of the beach, not far from the villa of my new occasional friend. He sometimes used to take advantage of this to come and exchange a couple of words with us, like a released prisoner visiting his cell mates. The boarders' crocodile passed just in front of his house, so on the day of the invitation, while we were playing ping-pong in his garden, under an umbrella pine whose extraordinarily bent trunk showed that the wind had been coming from the same direction for forty years (even though it doesn't always blow off the sea),

I heard my name yelled over the hedge by the whole gang, accompanied by somewhat disturbing remarks.

I would gladly have changed places, though. Having to fall over yourself to be polite and do the right thing, when you're afraid of making a faux pas and feel you're under surveillance, is already no sinecure, but the trouble with people who have money is that they have everything, including a ping-pong table. And ping-pong was far from being my speciality. Not having played it very often, my difficulty was twofold: in the first place, to try to reach the balls my opponent gently sent me, and then to send them back over the net, hoping they would land on his side. Some will object that these are the most elementary rules of the game. No doubt, but only in theory. Reaching the ball depended entirely on the skill (the very real skill, he ought to be world champion) of my opponent, who generously made every effort (he was a boy scout in civilian life) to aim at the centre of my bat. But if I held my bat parallel to the table, the balls bounced off its rim, which sent them back in most whimsical trajectories: one climbed up and took refuge in the crown of the umbrella pine and, offended no doubt, refused to come down. But this was an exceptional case. In general, I had enough space between the top of the net and the lowest branches in order not to exhaust the supply of balls provided by the house.

This didn't prevent my friend from seeming to be highly satisfied with my services. At lunchtime, after a rapid meeting and when we had already played three games in rather less than ten minutes, he confided to his mother, who was a bit worried about my gifts, that I had put up quite a resistance, and that he had had to fight hard to win the last game by twenty-one to three. Which will give some idea of how eagerly I was awaiting the return game.

In my defence – I was playing with only one eye. The lens in my glasses had broken just a few days earlier and I had preferred to wait until the next holidays to get a replacement. I was afraid that the fog I would have been condemned to while my glasses were being repaired might expose me to various embarrassments, for example a malicious Authority, aware of my infirmity, might shout at me: What am I reading? tapping with his delicate bamboo pointer at a beastly mathematical formula chalked on the board and, in the absence of any answer (for, in spite of the way the question was formulated, he wouldn't have been addressing this injunction to himself), enjoining me to copy it out a hundred thousand times, as he hastened to rub it out. So I followed the lessons with one eye, the blurred vision of the other being entangled in the nylon thread, now twisted into a figure of eight while waiting for another lens for it to support.

The moment I got out of the classroom I took off my half-glasses and gradually learnt, at the cost of some embarrassing mix-ups, to follow the ecliptic disc of the football in our games, to seem to be lost in thought to avoid greeting an unidentifiable figure in the distance (that's to say more than three metres away), to avoid straining my eyes by screwing them up (which gives you a headache and makes you look half-witted), to be content with this approximation of the world, trying to persuade myself that I wasn't losing so very much and that not everything ("There is no new thing under the sun") was worth looking at.

But for the ping-pong game, after a fruitless attempt, which had got me again and again slapping the air with my bat, while my anxious friend was pointing out that the little white ball had gone over to the other side, I had to resign myself to putting my Cyclopean frames back on. Which faced me with a tragi-classical dilemma: as our games after lunch included a spectator (the champion's sister, a year older, and of intimidating beauty – long, chestnut-coloured hair, dark eyes, the figure of a world-champion ballerina, her feet poised in the ten-to-two position), which was better? to be ridiculous without glasses by missing the ball, or to be ridiculous with my half-frames on my nose, knowing that my talents at table-tennis, even with half-improved vision (I could only play forehand, but it was useless for my friend to serve to me on my good side as it was also the side of the missing lens, hence several missed shots), would probably not be great enough to dazzle her? It was a daring but brilliant stroke that made me opt for the second solution (one of the three points I had won in the last game of the morning was when a ball rebounded from the tip of the handle of my bat, scraped the net and wrong-footed my opponent). Observing that with a bit of practice my game was improving, I was hoping to play a few more shots like that one, watched by the beauty, and to get my bat to produce, like a conjuror from his sleeve, a sort of final flourish, crowned by a smash such as no one had ever seen, which would get her jumping up and flinging herself into my arms to kiss the winner, even if the loser was her brother, which, still from the tragi-classical point of view, didn't present an insuperable obstacle, seeing that Chimène had fallen into a pair of arms one of which that very same morning – which shows considerable broadmindedness on her part – had killed her father.

Seen from Random, via Saint-Cosmes, she had the elegance and simplicity of the fashionable districts: navy blue skirt, pale blue blouse, a scarf knotted boy-scout fashion round her neck, but this must actually have been the uniform of the girl guides, with whom she had spent the morning and part of the afternoon. Still imbued with the necessity of doing a good deed every day, she chased after my lost balls which she brought back with a smile, and which I took from her with a permanent blush, not having time to turn white again between one ball and the next and, as I couldn't imagine that she had been running around like that because she had been entranced by my baby brown eyes (difficult to see behind my one-eyed frames), I could only think that she was seizing this opportunity to get in a stock of good deeds and accumulate enough to last for at least a year.

In my personal opinion, sticking my nose against the mirror, and in so far as it is possible to be your own best judge, I rather had the impression that my physique gained by not being lumbered with those horrible thick-lensed glasses, and therefore that when I took them off I was stacking up a few winning cards in my hand, with regard, I mean, to the agonising question: Will a girl ever be interested in me? which is the sole, the one and only question, in comparison with which all others seem insignificant, even the fate of the planet, on condition, of course, that it doesn't affect the response to the aforesaid question. (Hence the tests of the order of: If I manage to get my service in all right it'll be settled, we shall live happily ever after, and as for children, it's still a bit early to think about them. And that's where, with so much at stake, the hand trembles: And what if by any chance I don't get my service in? Alone for life just for a ball in the net? That would be enough to make you despair of determinism in general and of God in particular, so let's take our precautions, don't let's be stupid enough to mortgage our future love life on a bad shot, don't let's try to make an impression, let's play safe and forget about style: bat nice and flat over the table, hit the ball from top to bottom at a slight angle so it bounces off and clears the net by a good metre. So far everything is going swimmingly, and now, provided the shot isn't too long, twist your neck to alter the trajectory from a distance, there are just a few centimetres in it, but phew! the ball lands on the table. I already can't wait to know the name of my betrothed, and what she's going to be like, even though I admit that a beauty like her, bending down for the n*th* time to look for the lost ball that I didn't see coming, just revealing a little of her ballerina's thighs which are already tanned by the Atlantic iodine and sun, with or without an intact pair of glasses, doesn't enter into my field of vision.)

But the others were well aware of it; when they saw me without glasses they never missed a chance to ask me why I didn't wear them any more, and whether it was simply out of vanity, to make myself interesting in the eyes of you know who. And here it seems to you that the world really is cruel, that it doesn't make any effort to put itself in your place which, from your point of view, couldn't be more hopeless, never knowing what to do or what expression to adopt – but in any case, a different one – for who on earth could be interested in you the way you actually are?

The lady who keeps the Random pâtisserie, where every Sunday morning we buy five cakes; four, now, since the one who liked chocolate éclairs left us in the lurch – but Mother likes to keep up this ritual, she wants life to go on as before, which is to say at least a sort of facsimile of it – takes (perhaps as a sign of bad temper: our choice always falls on the same cakes, even though she urges us to try her new lines, but in vain, hence her lament: Whatever is the use of making innovations, this stick-in-the-mud attitude of country people, ah, if only she was in a town) a perverse pleasure in asking how it happens that my glasses haven't been mended yet. Shouldn't I change opticians, actually she knows one, and I would ruin my eyes and end up like her uncle, for instance, last month a cornea operation, all the time arranging the cakes in the little white lidless cardboard box she has folded and is about to wrap in tissue paper. But you've already stopped listening. Why do people prevent you from looking to advantage? Who does it inconvenience? Oughtn't they rather to encourage anyone who is aspiring to happiness? Do I tell her that if I were she I would have arranged the cakes differently, all the more so as four are easier than five; five have to be piled up, with an almond tart supporting a cream puff, which is better than the other way round.

But it's a fact, it's a conspiracy: some people conspire to spoil your pleasure. In Random, the only ones to escape from the dull, narrow, unimaginative framework imposed by local life are the old maids once they've gone a bit barmy who, after an existence steeped in piety, take to wearing hats from a bygone age, to playing at being starlets, and are always lifting up their skirts. The name the local people give them is not very original: they simply call them the madwomen. Through them, you realise that you mustn't miss the bus. It's only much later, looking at the war memorial with its impressive list of their potential fiancés killed between 1914 and 1918, that you tell yourself you would be well advised not to mistake one period of time for another and that they, the martyrs of History, never really had a chance. If you consider the men of marriageable age, it was a bloodletting, a veritable headache for marriage bureaux: there must be at least one out of every two absent from the roll call. But this gave the edge to the ones who came back; they could take their pick. So the strategy was simple: a war to eliminate some of the men, and fix things so as to be among the ones who come back. I increased my chances. I imagined my friend's sister as a dedicated nurse, bustling about among the wounded, elegant in her white veil, twirling around in her diaphanous dress, and anyway, that could well be the ideal solution: a minor injury which shows you aren't a coward, and get yourself nursed by the beauty. The difficult consisted in flushing out an understanding enemy who could aim accurately: just a simple graze on the top of the skull, and my friend's sister's hands, with infinite care, will be making you a turban which testifies that you have faced the enemy.

That same evening she appeared in my reveries. Because of her first aid, and the other kind act at teatime when she had asked me what I would like on my bread and butter, jam or hazelnut cream and, flustered, incapable of deciding and still blushing, I had mumbled that I didn't mind and, when she insisted, had been appalled to hear myself answer, as if ectoplasm was issuing from my mouth: Both, with the result that a little later, with a smile, she handed me a world-première slice of bread, red and brown. A smile that I immediately interpreted as meaning something like: I knew that my brother's friend whom he had never mentioned before today was an idiot, with his half-glasses on his nose and his pathetic shoestring dangling over his right eye, but, if he's as far gone as that, does he really think he will be able to carry on with his studies? And I imagined them after I had left, the two of them, brother and sister, remimicking the scene (the hybrid slice of bread and my affected mannerisms), playing it over and over again, each time convulsed by the same shrieks of laughter. But I had my revenge: I had noticed that she bit her nails, which, in my eyes, detracted from her kind of beauty, and to a certain extent made up for my awkwardness and my patched-up glasses. Which is why, that evening, I permitted myself to embed her in my reveries, those that precede the dive into sleep, in which you can call your own tune.

Until the lights finally went out (there were twenty switches in a double row in the supervisor's alcove, and for a long time their successive clicks were the reveille signal), we had no peace. Silence was the rule in the dormitory, to break it was to risk the usual punishments (although, after a hard day that had started very early, most of the boys, including the hotheads, were merely longing for sleep). But we had invented a method of communicating by putting our heads in our lockers under the windows, once we had noticed that the central heating pipes ran along the bottom of them, and this enabled us to use them as improvised confessionals where we could exchange a few remarks vital to our survival: Fraslin is a nutcase, or: Do you reckon Juju is blind in his squinty eye? or: What was it again that the sum of the angles of a triangle is equal to? But of course this game was not all that unobtrusive: two boarders with their heads in their respective and adjoining lockers for five minutes, naturally that looked a bit fishy. So one of them was requested to go and kneel in the corner of the alcove by the lavatories, and the other to spend part of the night outside the dormitory door on the landing which, in the winter, was glacial.

In the winter, too, since we abbreviated the time of our ablutions, making sparing use of the rough and ready sanitary facilities (a horizontal pipe, fastened to the wall every fifty centimetres by a couple of little brackets, from which a thin trickle of cold water flowed into a white-enamelled metal basin, a sort of trough that was too high for the smaller boys to put a leg in), it sometimes happened that the Authority, having undertaken the inspection of the feet of an alleged suspect, and even though we were already in bed, would send us all back to wash, so that even after lights out it was a good idea not to start your dream machine going until you had made sure that nothing would come and disrupt it.

All this time, down below, the sea was indefatigably hurling its rollers against the concrete breakwaters, expiring on the beach, retreating in a turbulent confusion of pulverised shells before mounting a fresh attack, never discouraged, always heavy with suppressed rage, the obstinate white front line of the waves once again launching an attack against the pebbles, driving back the fringe of seaweed, and then, worn out by so much effort, withdrawing to its rear. But this perpetual movement, this sonic companionship that lulled our nights all year long, was only a sort of preparation, a warming-up exercise for the great winter manoeuvres, when the storms raging over the Atlantic were such that we were convinced that the liquid hordes were going to sweep everything away with them.

At the high equinoctial tides the breakers came crashing over the embankment, cleared the little stone wall and burst on the pavement in two stages: first the main body of the wave, then, in a sort of delayed action, a volley of spray which seemed to come from the seeds of the sea, light, muffled, cascading, to close the sequence. In the course of these repeated assaults it was as if the waves were challenging each other: to keep pushing this mobile frontier between the elements farther forward, to gain more and more ground, to see which could land farthest away, so why not try to reach the caretaker's lodge, that little building with its four-sided slate roof squeezed between the two big symmetrical buildings on the seafront? This meant imitating champion acrobats and performing a western roll over the embankment, the pavement and the road, and then each wave, stung into action, gathers momentum, takes a running jump, arches its back and digs deep, shifting, menacing furrows in this brackish expanse of sand, the sea advancing like the wind through a cornfield, the crest of the waves becoming white, frothing, swelling, until it arrives at the obstacle, when a great wall of water breaks away from the swell and, with a prodigious thrust, triumphs over the stone rampart and hurls a liquid arch over the road.

With the bedclothes pulled up to our eyes, we listen to the preparation and development of these operations. There is a deafening din, an amalgam of the roar of the sea, the rumbles of the thunder, the lightning streaking through the dormitory and, on some nights, when the light from the street lamps seems enveloped in a bale of cotton wool, the deep, melancholy moan of the foghorns. On other evenings it's the rain which suddenly changes its nature and, from being merely a discreet presence, starts lashing at the windows as if an aberrant sandman, fed up with simply sprinkling individual grains in the eyes of the would-be sleepers, had thought up the idea of chucking whole shovelfuls of gravel up at the windows to knock us all out at one go. But the glass resists, so at the moment when the wave submerges the roof of the lodge, which reverberates like a drum, I am already out of reach, far away from the dormitory and the tempest, from the terrors of the day and the never-ending humiliations, taking refuge in a world of pure consolation and kindness, protected from fury and malevolence, a world against which no one, and not even the unbridled elements, can do a thing.

And tonight I have a guest: my friend's sister has come and joined me in a log cabin specially built at the top of a tree on an island where, hidden away from the rest of the world, we can snuggle up to each other. My imagination of love goes no further than daring kisses on the mouth, and I am content with long, tender embraces, soft words and an exchange of looks. To satisfy the needs of my internal cinema I have done a little touching up: I have made myself a head taller so as to be able to look into my beloved's eyes without having to stand on tiptoe, and of course I am sharp-sighted, which dispenses me from wearing glasses. (So I am reduced to re-inventing the horizon, replacing a sort of comatose jumble by a clear line like a razor slash at the place where the sky is supposed to join the water – but this is a purely formal construction which isn't of the slightest use to me, for my guest would never be so indelicate as to point into the distance and ask me: Do you see what I see?) I am also wearing white moccasins, which I thought looked very chic on the feet of a senior boy in the final year who was crossing the school playground with a long, buoyant stride (I tried, not very successfully, to imitate it, pushing off with my back leg the way they never stopped explaining to us in gym, conscientiously rolling my foot from heel to toe, but probably with the wrong momentum, and the result was that it became a vertical force that turned every step into a kind of goat's leap, which gave me the springy sensation of walking on the surface of the moon in slow motion).

As for her, she has stopped biting her nails, so now I can paint them with a beautiful red varnish which makes her look like a woman. I even had the idea of adding a faint touch of blue eyeshadow to her lids, but on the whole she is perfectly recognisable. It is still the same girl who picked up my stray ping-pong balls and gave me a hybrid slice of bread and butter. She is still wearing her navy blue skirt and pale blue blouse. I don't yet dare to undress her. Even in my dreams, at the very moment when I am stretching out a hand, I find a way to blush. Soon, when we are more intimate, after all those evenings clinging to each other in the half-light of the dormitory, cradled by the to-ing and fro-ing of the waves, I shall take advantage of it to swell her budding breasts a little but without changing her blouse, and this will make a bit of a bulge between the third and fourth buttons.

But, as time passes, her features fade. To reconstruct them I await another invitation, which never comes. It's a different friend, also a day boy whom I know just as little, who takes over. This one is the intergalactic ping-pong champion, but he hasn't got a sister so I am obliged to pick up my stray balls myself and, as we play in a cluttered garage and they tuck themselves away in all kinds of places, the games last longer. Yet this one too seems to appreciate my role as sparring partner, since he is absolutely determined to see me again on the following Thursday. I can hear him saying: Oh mother, please do let my new friend come again, I so rarely have a chance to practise on high balls.

Heroic tales are told about friendship, admirable deeds, lifelong pledges, and explanations like Montaigne's about his loving friendship with Etienne de la Boétie: "Because it was he, because it was I", which don't throw much light on it but which do effectively seem to be its *sine qua non*, but from there to crossing a whole town and changing buses twice . . . His story didn't make sense. And just because seven years earlier he had invited me into his garden on the seafront to make me look ridiculous, ping-pong bat in hand . . . In the meantime, I had caught on to their game. Two right-thinking families had gone in for a sort of competition about me. A poor little boarder had just lost his father: a poor little recently-orphaned boy is a test sent by the Lord to try our Christian charity. Children, you must show proof of your courage and abnegation; even if this little peasant were to eat with his fingers it is our duty to invite him. And they lecture the older sister: Thou shalt be nice to him, thou shalt not laugh at his glasses, thou shalt pick up his lost balls, thou shalt give him his tea (and no doubt six other commandments of the same nature to make up the number).

And now, put yourself in the place of the second family, equally well-off, equally right-thinking, although vexed at having to have the idea suggested to them. Ah well, if that's how it is, *we* will invite him for two Thursdays running. The first family could have outbid them – three consecutive Thursdays – but the sister and brother had obviously called a halt. The sister says: That's all very well, but I'm not going to spend all my free time chasing after ping-pong balls for that four-eyed goon. The brother says: Might as well play against a blind wall, a wall does at least return the ball. And then, if it was only his clumsiness, adds the sister, but remember, dear brother, the episode of the bread and butter. And the two of them are once again reduced to fits of uncontrollable laughter.

In the end they must have exhausted the delights of this far-off afternoon, but now here comes the brother, who had committed himself to long years of studying medicine but was already complaining of the boredom of his new milieu (he should have chosen literature), having crossed the town and then gone a bit farther (the arts faculty was stuck away on the outskirts, in the middle of a piece of waste land near the racecourse, and the hall of residence was farther still), to ask you how you're getting on and to lay in a stock of the latest gossip. And as people never escape from their milieu, it was more of a laboratory assistant, a budding Pasteur, who came to enquire about the reactions of his favourite cultural breeding ground within closed walls: that's to say in a cell, four metres by two, containing a single bed, a table-cum-desk with a cream-coloured formica top, an imitation-leather chair stuffed with chunks of foam rubber, (but given the exiguity of the room you might just as well sit on the bed when you're working at the table, that's if you like sitting low and writing with your nose on the page – in case of any problems with your eyesight, for instance), and in the entrance – separated from the room proper by a semi-partition of imitation mahogany – equipped with a wash-basin and a bidet (the blue, Butagaz-type gas ring on the shelf above the mirror being the property of the tenant, as is the little enamel saucepan – cream-coloured outside, white inside – which he mainly uses for heating the water for his teabags).

Do you know, dear sister, that no sooner had I stepped into his room than he looked at me as if I had been sent by the KGB or the Saint-Cosmes Old Boys' Association? You might have thought he had something to hide. And he probably did, at that, judging by his reaction when he saw me. There weren't any other chairs so I sat down on his bed, whereupon he immediately began to gather up the papers lying on his table and stuff them in an orange folder. I didn't have time to read its title, but it was a hyphenated first name, something like Etienne-Marcel (but what an odd idea to take an interest in a fourteenth-century guildmaster!), and it was complete with a very stylised, not to say perfunctory pen-and-ink drawing of a couple seen from behind, which he shoved into a briefcase, the one I remember him having at school, and anyway I've already mentioned it to you. It's a mouse-grey, heavy leather case with gussets, which he says used to belong to his father who was a commercial traveller and so needed a solid, roomy bag for his files, dossiers, catalogues and so on. And after his death his son immediately appropriated it on the pretext that it would be just the thing for carrying all his school books, etc. Because, as you may remember, if we forgot any of our books, punishments were handed out right and left, and the boarders had to think about this every morning, to check their timetable for the day, which they often stuck or pinned inside their desk lids, and to take everything they needed with them – during the day they weren't allowed into the study room, where their pigeonholes were. And so he, to keep out of that sort of trouble – just imagine, whenever you forgot something you had to sit with your arms folded throughout the lesson, and weren't allowed even to glance at your neighbour's book. (I remember one occasion when something even more cruel happened to him, and yet he hadn't left the Fables of La Fontaine behind, because we'd been told we would need them for the test on clause analysis, but believe it or not, instead of getting us to study a fable, what was his name again, Praslin or Fraslin, gave us a text to analyse – and this is why our friend saw it as a kind of conspiracy against him, and he may well not have been wrong – taken from the introduction, but he didn't have the same edition as the rest of the class, and therefore didn't have the same introduction, the result being that Praslin or Fraslin, who had merely given us the number of a page, referred him to the list that had been distributed at the beginning of the school year of the books we had to have, and refused, although it would have been perfectly simple, to lend him his own copy, so he got a zero just because his parents had thought it would be stupid to buy a second book of Fables when his older sister had already studied them, no doubt reckoning that no one was going to amuse himself by making any changes in the fables between one edition and another) – and that was why, as he did often forget something or other, either because he was absent-minded or maybe thinking about something else, and as he had got fed up with accumulating punishments and hours of detention because of his forgetfulness, he had had the idea of cramming the entire contents of his pigeonhole into what after all was his inheritance, but that briefcase was too weighty an inheritance for him and, as he was very small at the time, he had to bend his arm so as not to drag it along the ground (not his arm, which was well proportioned, but the briefcase), with the result that he was treated to some sarcastic remarks from the older boys and the teachers, who called him a snail or a tortoise: Why didn't he take his bed with him while he was about it? and his wardrobe? But he, carrying his heavy burden, on the verge of tears (you couldn't say a thing to him, he used to cry all the time, and what's more he was extremely touchy), answered them as best he could, for instance that, thanks to his method, not only had he not copped a single line for forgetting something, but the others had often been more than pleased to find things they needed in his holdall – and sometimes quite simply an ink cartridge for a fountain pen – and so before criticising it was better to think twice, or that kind of argument. But when I saw him again, still with the same gigantic briefcase, I also saw us again, dear sister, round the ping-pong table, and I remembered how we laughed. And anyway, you must have made a hell of an impression on him that day. After all these years, he asked after you, wanted to know what had become of you, and there I was a bit disconcerted, I replied – put yourself in my place – that I had no idea. What's that, I had no idea? So I said: In heaven, maybe. And at that, he stared at me, and it was *his* eyes that filled with tears. In that respect he hasn't changed, he's still the same weeping willow, and yet he must be eighteen now, since we are the same age. So it was *I*, which seemed a bit much, who had to comfort *him*. That softened him at once and he offered me a cup of tea, excusing himself for having nothing else to offer me. I refused, on the pretext that I had already disturbed his work quite enough, but he maintained that even though appearances were against him he hadn't been working. He went to all the lectures but never took notes, so he had nothing to revise and he hadn't in fact been revising. He must have got into that habit after he gave up wearing glasses. (Good heavens, do you remember? every time we saw a dustbin, we said: Ah, his glasses' case.) As he couldn't read what was written on the blackboard, even when he was sitting in the front row, he had decided that the lessons would take place without him – with him, but without him. How, under such conditions, did he ever manage to pass the exams in maths, physics and chemistry, when, as we know, at the end of an hour's lesson the boards are covered with demonstrations and formulas that you absolutely have to learn and remember? This is a mystery which makes me doubt his alleged myopia. He maintains that he was lucky, and that that was why, knowing he would never have such luck twice, he switched to literature. In the meantime, shortsighted or not, I told him that when I arrived I had nevertheless found him hard at work. No no, he insisted, against all appearances. Hadn't he been writing? Yes, of course, but it was something quite different. Then I remembered that at Saint-Cosmes he had got himself a bit of a reputation as a versifier, he could write a hundred alexandrines making fun of a supervisor, or compose a sonnet about the rain. He had even, after the unfortunate experience I have told you about, written a fable in the style of La Fontaine, whose moral was something like: The moral? There are no more morals. I remember this because he had got caught, because Praslin or Fraslin had read out the text in class, but stopped just before the last line and written on the board: Moral: Clause analysis of Book I of the Fables of La Fontaine.

Without reminding him of this episode, then, I asked him whether he was still writing.

AND SO MY FIRST love had drowned. Yet she was a good swimmer. Which just goes to show that the sea is no good, not even for the fish. It had engulfed her ballerina's body, then returned it to her family a few days later, cast up unceremoniously like a dead branch, a bottle, or a piece of orange peel, on to the very same beach where we used to organise our long-jump competitions and where for a long time I had hoped that after we had met, prompted by a desire to see me again and knowing that this was the destination of our walks, she would come and join me. Spreading out her towel not far from our group, rubbing herself with suntan lotion, and from time to time darting an admiring glance at my celestial flights (not being able to show off my dribbling skills in the sand, I chose to keep goal), she would have brought me back the rubber ball which I had accidentally on purpose allowed to elude me, in spite of a magnificent dive designed less to prevent the opposing team from scoring than to make it land like a tribute at her ballerina's feet. A ball which I don't want to send back, now that it is slightly imbued with the perfumed lotion covering her arms, her legs, her shoulders (she is far too well brought-up to ask for the help she might possibly need to oil her back), which I am hugging very tightly to my chest, as if it were a part of her, but actually everyone has lost all interest in the game now that our favourite spectator is crossing the beach in her two-piece swimsuit, navy blue bottom and sky-blue top, based on her girl guide uniform, tossing her long hair back and then plunging head first into the rollers, emerging a few metres farther out until, exerting her arms, she disappears from our sight.

And that was how the sea had swallowed her up during her sixteenth summer, while she was swimming offshore, alone, and had probably suddenly got cramp. She must have called out in vain, perhaps trying to attract the attention of the little group of boarders playing on the beach. But her gesticulations, her cries would have been completely useless: even in my reveries I never went to the aid of a drowning woman. What's the use, when you can't swim.

I would have liked to ask my friend whether he had a photo of my siren-ballerina on him. Her features had become permanently blurred, and all I could remember was her long hair – except for a faint memory of her navy skirt and the little bit of her thighs I glimpsed when she bent over to look for my lost balls in the tall grass in the garden, but that wasn't necessarily a genuine memory. It was possible that other, later, visions had been grafted on to this childish image; skirts blown up over an air vent, for instance, that the cinema, via the television, which my family acquired a few years later, had relayed. It was even more difficult for me to make the blurred face of the drowned girl a few years older by stopping on the verge of her sixteenth year, that's to say the extreme limit of childhood which already presages the emergent woman.

I had worked so hard, evening after evening, in the light dusk of the dormitory, at making a photofit picture of her, updating it as time went by and her features lost resolution, no doubt preparing myself, by this wrong-way-round face-lift for our next meeting for which, being more mature, I granted myself a second chance, so that when I was taking the orange folder out of my briefcase at my friend's request I had no option but to admit that that clumsily-drawn silhouette seen from behind – that was still her, so she had unconsciously survived her dissolution and the accumulation of my reveries. A young woman with long flowing hair coming down to her waist, giving her arm to a young man wearing tails and a top hat rakishly tilted over his ear, his right hand holding the neck of a bottle of spirits which could have been Armagnac, round and flat, but which, given the clumsy way it was drawn, could just as well have been a ping-pong bat.

For, officially, the young man in evening dress appeared to be a clone of Rimbaud (the model was supposed to recall Delahaye's fanciful sketches which showed his friend taking long strides over the whole world), which the title rendered in a manner that was not much more explicit: Jean-Arthur or The Same Thing. An equally vague allusion to what drinkers say, i.e. The Same Again (here meaning: If I had my time again I'd do the same thing), so it should be understood that the said Jean-Arthur had survived the amputation of his leg (which in the drawing was replaced by a wooden leg, Captain Ahab or Long John Silver style), and I explained to my friend that, on his return home (women tend to look after these ferocious disabled people, etc.), he had been reunited with the sister of one of his childhood friends, who had dreamed of this adventurer about whom her brother was constantly talking, and one day while they were sitting together on a park bench he had wanted to dazzle her with tales of his adventures and, having no qualms about stretching the truth, he had added:

Africa, the heat, the desert, the cannibals, the lions, the slave traffic, the soil in the sacks of coffee, the beautiful Abyssinian girls, and she, ingenuous, attentive, had said: Why don't you write a book about it? I remember that my brother copied out a sonnet on the rain, whose first line began: Rain is a companion. Didn't *you* write that? And when the presumed poet replied: Hogwash, all that was nothing but hogwash, I felt myself blushing, and the brother of the beautiful drowned girl noticed my embarrassment, but instead of coming to my aid he looked at his watch and said: I won't keep you any longer, and then added something like: Be that as it may, you know now how the story ends. With these words he stood up, abruptly confessed that he probably wouldn't complete his medical studies either, that he felt like packing it all in and becoming a shepherd. What? A shepherd? and instead of leaving it at that, with this flabbergasted exclamation, you try to be clever and you add: At the rate vocations are going, there's soon going to be a shortage of sheep, which makes him smile for a quarter of a second – any longer than that would have constituted an exercise in compassion which was visibly beyond him – just time for him to turn round and put his hand on the doorknob.

AND NOW YOU ARE once again alone in your room, whose window consists of two aluminium-framed sliding panels and looks out on to other similar blocks, an agglomeration of cells all identical to this one, infinitely repetitive architecture rehashing the same unlovely motif, a poem consisting of the same pathetic line reproduced a thousand times over. After your friend has left, you wonder whether you haven't missed a good opportunity and whether, rather than suspecting just about everyone of being a spy, you shouldn't perhaps get it into your head that there do also exist disinterested pledges of friendship, such as crossing a town and changing buses twice simply to come and see how you are and sing out, loud and clear: What's new? and the answer could of course be: This and that, but in the meantime it's good to see you, and anyway I've been meaning to make the same journey in reverse.

Because this, so it seems, is something that is done, quite simply and without ulterior motive. That's why you feel so helpless at not being able to perform such elementary acts, when in fact you envy those groups of young people who get together, drink, laugh, kiss, travel, break up, and then get together again. However much you adopt a superior, disdainful expression and affect total incomprehension of this kind of collective behaviour, you would nevertheless give a lot to be able to join them, which at that age seems to be the norm, instead of staying alone in your little corner stringing phrases together, finding rhymes for songs, and, bending over a fashionable musical instrument, dreaming of fabulous tomorrows when the situation will be blissfullly reversed (the last shall be first), and you will delight in the knowledge that your name is engraved in the hearts of the masses.

But for the moment you are still trying to convince yourself that it was a bit of luck that your offer of tea was refused: if it had already been drunk, you would have been deprived of your only recourse. This unceremonious tea ceremony in the middle of your day represents a quarter of an hour salvaged, snatched from sadness and solitude, a collection of little acts which, methodically pieced together, temporarily dispel the feeling of boredom that never leaves you: the water poured into the cream-coloured saucepan, chosen for its reduced format (the smallest model, the one that fits into the very top of a stack of saucepans), the match you strike which you hold up to your lips and delicately blow out once it has ignited the burner on the stove, the familiar hiss of the gas under pressure, the crown of blue flames like a tenacious little cushion against the premature invasion of winter darkness, the little clinking sound of the saucepan being put down on the metal grid, the teabag waiting in the straight-sided china mug with the coral-pink border round the rim, its label hanging outside (if it happens to slide into the cup while you're pouring the bubbling water out of the saucepan it turns it red and yellow, or even golden brown, more or less the colour of the tea, which is preferable to a green or blue dilution, but the most simple and effective way to avoid this nuisance is to twist the thread joining the tea bag to its label round the handle of the mug. As this ritual would lose all meaning if you just casually plonked the mug down on a corner of the table, for it is essential for it to be emphasised, to be apprehended with the greatest possible intensity, the central area of the desk has first been cleared, its books and papers removed, and a white towel has been unfolded to serve as a table cloth. Every move is calculated so as to gain a handful of seconds, as for instance the particular way of testing with the tips of the lips, no hurry, your nose plunged into the cloud of steam rising from the cup, the temperature of the tea, and then drinking it in tiny sips, not so much for the pleasure it gives you, it really isn't the best-quality tea, but because you feel that this way you are keeping time at a distance, and its insidious drip, drip, drip, and its art of the void.

But time knows how to defend itself. It is compressible – but only up to a point. A kind of Boyle's law applied to its passing prevents you from using it as you wish. It doesn't do you the slightest good to drag out each movement of this ritual as far as it will go, or even to overheat your water so it takes longer to cool; in the end, when the last sip has been swallowed and the cup washed up, no more than fifteen minutes have ever passed, and we still have a long way to go until the evening meal. A vast two-hour interval stretches out in front of you that you really don't know how to fill, during which you move from your table to your bed, from writing three words which you immediately cross out to playing the same chords on your guitar, although they have become infuriating through constant repetition. For nothing lasts, boredom submerges everything – including your reveries.

That blessed space at the frontier of the night, which alleviated your school years, has lost its power to console, now that the gift of time aplenty and the absence of constraints have made its use a commonplace. At times you have even rebelled against the forces of the imagination, like Michelangelo cursing his Moses, you have wept with rage at its useless products. Solitude has no equal in rendering things futile.

The previous year, the last one at Saint-Cosmes, taking advantage of a liberalisation of the regime (the transition, for final-year boarders, from the dormitory to their own room), you secretly started to learn to play the guitar, like ninety per cent of your age group (the remaining ten per cent had had piano lessons as part of their education). The below-average marks you got during that year show how much that musical craze, substituting itself for the study of mathematics, cost you. But when all's said and done it wasn't very much, in comparison with the paradoxical joy of being unusual in the same way as everyone else, of escaping your inner exile and getting outside yourself. Which was what you had had a slight taste of in the days when your ironical alexandrines, kind of intrepid Samizdats mocking the tics of the school authorities and their foibles, used to circulate behind the raised lids of our desks and for which your peers granted you the special status of semi-official poet. But for verse, all you have to do is count on your fingers, and only up to twelve, the words come tumbling out of their own accord, push and shove each other, pass auditions, all you have to do is pick and choose. Finally, and whatever people say here or there, it's no big deal. Whereas to manage to produce dulcet tones from six metal strings that lacerate the tips of your fingers to the point where they end up growing calluses, if there is no grandeur in this musical tenacity, there is at least merit. You place your index finger on a particular fret, a particular string, your middle finger on this or that other one, and then your ring finger, and when your little finger joins in you have a choice of four or five more variations, all this at the cost of painful cramps in your poor thumb, unseen under the neck, which is acting as a clamp.

And this is merely for your left hand. But your right hand doesn't wish to be outdone, even if to start with it is content to come crashing down like a scythe on the surface of the six strings, rhythmically if possible, postponing the moment when you have to start its fingers picking, pecking, knitting, knotting. The main thing is to produce a homogeneous sound which doesn't give the impression of having been made by a flat-tyred old bicycle, squeaking and ironmongering. And now that your four blood-stained left-hand fingers can manage to produce a virtually perfect chord, so much so that you never tire of playing it again and again, it's also the sign that it's time to do something else, if you want to play pieces that are not essentially repetitive. And this is where everything becomes complicated. Take two chords: king and kong, for example. If, after you have played king, kong doesn't follow immediately, there'll always be some fellow with big ears to observe that you have no sense of rhythm. So you get a pal to do your physics homework for you, after which you merely have the trouble of copying it out, and during that time you keep on and on at it. Tring-trong, kring-dong, ding-vrong, and at last: king-kong.

There. You can play. At least well enough to go on to the next stage: the accompaniment, which is to say that with these same chords you now have a chance to sing – not at the top of your voice (anyone making his début as a singer has more of a tendency to start somewhat confidentially), but with a shrill, nasal twang – violently anti-authoritarian songs, devastating hymns which, by challenging the established order, do a great deal of damage to the property-owning classes.

To tell the truth, you only pay lip service to the former, they even embarrass you a little (their lack of subtlety, no doubt), but, so as not to remain permanently on the sidelines, you force yourself to chant the latest hit, an unattractive compromise which doesn't show any great courage, but solitude has become truly unbearable. And how can you explain, unless you want to be seen as a pathetic counter-revolutionary, that you really prefer sentimental songs, it's your romantic side, secretly culti-vated on the flower beds of the nights at Saint-Cosmes? And anyway, the moment you have a few chords at your fingertips, you start composing.

You've done it: in two-four time, three movements and a myriad of wrong notes: four love songs. But how, and by whom, are you going to get them heard? You suffer, don't forget, from pathological shyness, the sort that is no help at all when you have to make a public announcement of the order of: And now I am going to play you a song – words and music by me – (hint: this charming young man can do everything). The opportunity presents itself during a village fête in Random. Not on the stage of the actual theatre (a real one, Italian-style, with neither stucco nor gilding but with wings, flies and stage machinery), but just underneath it, that's to say under the boards on which enthusiastic young people are noisily treading, and this means that you can hear your colleagues on the floor above declaiming their lines, the girls in the corps de ballet prancing about, and the musicians – an English-inspired group – performing.

A charitable soul has dragged you there. Obviously charitable, because it must have taken some insistence before you condescended to agree (in your defence, you find it difficult to explain that your reluctance has no other reason than the fear and shame of looking silly and self-conscious, of being a killjoy, otherwise you would already have been there). Youth is a style, and it is only too obvious that you don't possess it. So you arrive in the wings of the theatre, after having vaguely waved to this one and that (who may well find this astonishing, when they remember that not so long ago you hadn't even deigned to wave back to them, not being able to imagine that from the other side of the road they only exist in your eyes within the category of probabilities, which is why you have got into the habit of lowering your head rather than blindly waving to hazy outlines who sometimes turn out to be perfect strangers, amazed at this greeting from someone they don't know – but you can already hear the comments behind your back: He's a lunatic, says hallo when he feels like it, at the drop of a hat). And you are delighted to find a guitar tucked away in a corner: at last something to show you to advantage, to make you look self-confident, to present you in a new and favourable light. And so, secretly hoping that people will notice you, your right foot on a straw-bottomed chair, your head bent over the strings, you started first by playing, and then by mumbling – (king) above the town a pall of rain/ (kong) my love is fragile and in vain – while the young artists are rushing around stage left and stage right, pushing and shoving, bumping into your elbow as they go past, and seem only moderately concerned with the fragility of your loves.

Finally, someone notices your talents, listens, and is certainly going to ask you who wrote that marvellous song, but, interrupting you without the slightest regard for your loves, he tells you that he would very much like to learn to play the guitar, couldn't you give him lessons? obliging you to reply that you taught yourself, but that if he insists you will give him a copy of the position of the fingers on the neck for king and kong, before indignantly going back to the beginning of your interrupted chanson (you are not one of those musicians who can carry on from the thirteenth bar as if nothing has happened). Then along comes a drum majorette, scared stiff at the idea of tripping over her feet in her dance steps, who sets about rehearsing under your very nose (which is in the strings), doing high kicks with alternate thighs, whose only direct consequence on your playing would have been an acceleration of your cardiac rhythm had she not, grabbing her baton, started twirling it between her fingers with great dexterity, whereupon, seeing your already fragile love in imminent danger of being knocked on the head, you decide on a strategic retreat to the floor below, you take your guitar and chair, descend the narrow, dusty stairs, and decide to take up your pitch not far from the prompt box, between the pillars supporting the stage.

You know this place by heart. You remember, now. Your old Aunt Marie was the person who filled in the gaps in the memories of the amateur actors, which meant that you and your sisters were privileged to sit beside her, taking turns on the white bench, and, with your eyes on a level with the stage, to watch the performances. One of them in particular impressed you: *The Escape of Saint Peter*, in which Saint Peter (played by a foreman from the dairy, outrageously made up, his eyes coal-black, his mouth and cheekbones emblazoned as if he was on the warpath, dressed in a short, ragged tunic cut out of a hessian sack), lying prostrate on the floor of the

Mamertine prison behind the circus railings, was making water gush up from a well in order to baptise his gaolers (a hosepipe propelled a powerful jet through a trap door, and the water then dripped down through the prompt box), before being delivered by two angels (one of whom was the postman, recognisable by his moustache which he hadn't been prepared to shave off for the occasion, being content to cover it with flesh-coloured powder). Therefore, thanks to your perfect knowledge of the place, due to it having been frequented by such indisputable playwrights as Georges Ohnet and Paul Féval, you start to sing your compositions (this must certainly be an all-time first in the history of the music hall: to appear underneath a stage to a full house without the said full house being aware that anything is going on), hoping that the ascending sound will squeeze its way up through the prompt box and charm the ears of the front rows or, failing that, of a drum majorette. With the English-inspired group following on and all their guitars being electrified, you soon abandon the struggle. Even if the pall of rain over the town is still coming down in bucketfuls that's no cause for alarm on the Atlantic seacoast, but your so fragile love has really had enough.

For grandmother, these few chords were enough to make me a musician. In her eyes, I was taking up the family torch which Grandfather had abandoned on his death, as none of his three daughters, to his great despair, had persevered with the study of her instrument. He had taught one the cello and the others the viola and the piano, and had always dreamed of forming a quartet, with himself taking the violin part. Grandmother had noticed in the course of her long life that passions and talents often skipped a generation and, as the people with whom she shared the fruits of her reflections seemed to be of the same opinion, you had to imagine a musical gene leap-frogging over the three girls and coming to rest, considerably weakened by this space–time leap, on the head of one of Alphonse's grandsons.

And so nothing is ever lost. This economical concept, wholly in line with the life principles obtaining in the family, had nevertheless to be seen in perspective when you passed from Mozart to king-kong. But after all, Grandmother could always attribute this decline to the new canons of modernity. And having heard me, or at least having caught a glimpse, in a prominent position on a kitchen chair, of the bargain guitar made of recycled wood which I held responsible for the defects in my playing, she decided that Grandfather's violin, which hadn't been out of its case for some ten years, was mine by right as it seemed that I had inherited his gifts. In her defence, Grandmother had never had an ear for music.

All her life she had pretended to have no interest in what had been her husband's great passion and a source of conflict between them. Her most famous act of rebellion was when she broke the flute of a commercial traveller who was playing a duet with Alphonse while one of her daughters was upstairs giving birth. She seemed in a hurry to get rid of all her late husband's musical mementos, because at the same time as the violin she handed over his entire collection of scores to me, and also his notebooks. Among these were manuals of fugue and counterpoint which he had studied at the Paris Conservatoire when, as a young man who had gone up to the capital to practise his talents as a tailor at the highest level and put the finishing touches to his apprenticeship, he took advantage of the occasion to add substance to his local violin prize. What this amounted to, where I was concerned, was bequeathing an encyclopaedia to an illiterate.

So, as I didn't know what to do with it, the violin remained for a long time in its case, a sort of little coffin in black wood, tapering, isosceles-shaped, its corners rounded, its lid in two sections surmounted by a folding copper handle, and fastened on the side by a couple of metal clasps. The whole thing would have stayed as it was, that's to say as one of those useless objects you don't dare get rid of because it's either too rare or too full of memories, if it hadn't been for a jingle I heard on the radio, the music to a Celto-Berrichon folk dance or something of the sort, a corny old tune jazzed up to suit present-day tastes, but which, to play it, would apparently not need long years of study at the Conservatoire, all the more so as on the sleeve of the record especially bought for the occasion (the group was posing round a hay cart drawn by a horse, itself wearing a Tyrolean hat), the girl violinist (long curly hair, loose-fitting smock, full skirt), standing perched on top of the sheaves, had solved the delicate problem of the classic way of holding the instrument (tucked between the chin and shoulder, which causes, apart from an unsightly goitre, a painful contraction of the tendons of the neck, and there is also the unpleasant contact of the sounding board on your clavicle – hence the pad or cloth used by some virtuosos) by positioning it directly over her bosom. But even without such a practical little cushion, this showed that you could extract some sort of sound out of this instrument without having had any official teaching, the golden rule simply being to play as fast as possible so as not to have to linger on any one note, which, without the vibration produced on the string by a Parkinsonian finger, then emits a long falsetto whine. For the rest, any fool can play more or less out of tune.

And it was to this end that I began to apply myself, in my room at the hall of residence, having first taken care to fix a mute on the bridge, considering, correctly no doubt, that the fleeces of our sheep, tra la, / 'tis we as wields the shears, / the fleeces of our sheep, baa baa, / 'tis we gets their wool, my dears. / was perhaps not to the taste of all my neighbours, who might well prefer Mozart, for example (i.e., the violin under the chin), or even silence, which is fairly appropriate to study, rather than hearing me endlessly returning to my sheep shearing. And even though I did my utmost to give my bucolic scales a jaunty little twist, a dancing aspect, I was all the time expecting protesting knocks on the wall or ceiling, so when they did in fact sound on my door I thought my sheep's last hour had come, which made me very sad because I had by no means come to the end of my shearing.

Of course I should have recognised him, in spite of his long hair and the intervening years, if only by that lens of his spectacles embedded in his eye-socket, which gave the impression that his ear on that side was set a little farther back than the other one, just a short centimetre out of line, perhaps, but, as there was nothing to be done about the length of the sidepiece (the frames being standard, all ages and both sexes), the lens was pulled back until it was clamped against his eye. And then that voice, obviously deeper, having broken since, but with exactly the same intonation, that rather common, surburban accent which drags out certain syllables, all the more surprising in that Gyf had never lived in a suburb, only in the country, or perhaps it was a leftover from his stay in the orphanage, the arrogant brashness of the outcast. But he hadn't come, like the brother of the drowned girl, for an attempt at a reunion of the old boys of Saint-Cosmes, or even to protest against the din. What interested *him*, was precisely the violin. So I had been right not to overdo the use of the mute. All the more so as he straightaway announced the reason for his visit: he might possibly need my services. Which flattered me, but once the moment of exultation had passed: who did he expect would believe any such thing? Who could possibly need *me*? I had been right to be suspicious. This place was crawling with spies. I wasn't so sorry, now, that I had so unceremoniously dispatched the ex-world-champion ping-pong player. Now they were sending me a pseudo-impresario.

Without even waiting for an invitation to sit down, he perched on the bed in the lotus position (actually, cross-legged, like a tailor, but people had just discovered the road to India), and exhorted me to resume my sheep shearing. What he was primarily interested in was to make sure that I played in time. This was a bit tricky. It was no good beating time with my foot, my foot was a partisan of my way of playing and certainly had no intention of amusing itself by suggesting any rhythmical modifications. It adapted itself and, as I had no other dancing partner, we, me and my foot, allowed ourselves a few liberties with the tempi. So this impromptu audition was not without risk.

I began by sticking the violin under my chin, to confuse the issue, and, bow in hand, began to unwind my balls of wool under the beady eye of my judge, who suddenly started slapping both hands down on the edge of the desk. Stop. He immediately remarked, after having got his fingers tangled up, that that wasn't it at all. I explained that for this kind of piece I had in fact been wrong to adopt the classic position, and, propping the violin up over my chest, observing in passing that it was not without reason that that was what all country fiddlers did, I begged him to give me another chance. The fleeces of our sheep, tra la, 'tis we as wields the shears, the fleeces of our sheep, baa baa, 'tis we gets their wool, my dears. The bow bounced off the strings, my left-hand fingers occasionally hit a right note, and this time the percussionist seemed satisfied. He stood up and, indicating by great swirls of his arm that I was to continue, adopted a becoming position, arched his back, and, hands on hips, launched into a few pirouettes in the narrow alley between the bed and the table, a faraway look in his eyes, occasionally tapping the floor with his foot, the shears, the shears, twisting around towards the window, 'tis we gets their wool, coming back, skilfully avoiding the corner of the bed, the shears the shears, tapping his foot more energetically, until he kicked the wastepaper basket over, 'tis we gets their wool, my dears, and decided that that was enough. But his try-out seemed conclusive: You can dance to it, he said, putting the crumpled bits of paper back into the basket. Among them, I recognised some heavily-corrected drafts of my Jean-Arthur.

He took advantage of this to ask me whether I had any other pieces in my repertoire. Well, *there* he was in luck. Taking the sheep and the jingle as my model, I had composed several tunes that gave the impression of coming straight from the Celto-Auvergnat melting pot, genuine fakes to which, while I was about it, I even suggested that I would write words, of equally guaranteed origin, if he liked. But actually, he didn't like; all he needed was a sound track for a short eight-millimetre film he had just made. Whereupon I began to understand his choice of glasses: I was dealing with an artist.

His film didn't have a subject – and I immediately regretted having asked about it – or rather, in the sense that it didn't tell a story. It was more a sort of allegory, if I saw what he meant. I saw, of course, but I was afraid of misinterpreting his thought, so I asked for a little clarification. I understood that to tell a story was a reactionary symptom whose purpose was to prevent the masses from becoming conscious of their condition as the exploited, while at the same time feeding them with counter-revolutionary models, but what about the images, wasn't there a risk that they might speak for themselves? In other words – and while I was quite prepared to recognise that the word images was perhaps not suited to his kind of film – people might perhaps see something in them. Precisely: an atmosphere. I immediately had a better grasp of my new friend's project, but, and I agreed that it was incorrect to insist, but an atmosphere of what? Did he use actors, for instance? Without waiting for his answer, though, I corrected myself: by actors, I meant participants. I prefer that, he said. I had had a narrow escape. Actually, he conceded, creation for him was primarily a chance to enjoy himself: making a film or making love was the same thing. So it wasn't a question of directing, in the Fascist sense of the word – here I protested: I would never have imagined such a thing, which he honestly believed – but of letting all the participants express, openly and without inhibitions, their own creative urges. It must be an interesting film, I opined. Interesting wasn't the word (no, of course it wasn't, but I really wasn't in possession of all my faculties that day), and in any case, to his mind the result was completely unimportant: for him, tightening a bolt or composing a Bach fugue was six of one and half a dozen of the other: it was only the act that counted, but at all events it was too early to know, as he himself had not yet seen his film.

This proof was enlightening; since the result was completely unimportant, he hadn't even taken the trouble to view it. This act-non-act was also a part of the creative act. Furthermore, to be interested in your own work came into the category of self-interest and hence of profits, coupled with petit-bourgeois self-satisfaction. I was very pleased, dialectically speaking, to be able to show that I was beginning to understand a thing or two, when he stopped me: he was two-hundred per cent in agreement with me, but it was nevertheless his duty to explain that if he hadn't seen his film, that was because it hadn't yet been developed. It would cost a fortune to print the negative, and at the moment he was broke. However, he was counting on some money coming in soon: a collection of family silver had been discovered in the attic of a girlfriend's grandmother, and he was proposing to sell it at the flea market. And once this had been achieved, would I get a chance to see it? That went without saying, otherwise he wouldn't be here. But before explaining my part to me – aha, so I was going to be in it? – he asked me whether I didn't perhaps have something to drink? Only tea. My casting director made a face. He suggested we might stroll round to the café on the corner (the corner actually being a good kilometre away from the hall of residence).

THE SAID CAFÉ WAS called *Au Bon Pêcheur,* a memory from the time when it had been outside the town and there had been a river which attracted keen anglers. The river had been partly filled in, partly turned into a sewer, and the town had gradually crept up on the tavern, which owed its survival only to the establishment of an open-air university mainly consisting of bungalows scattered here and there in the middle of the woods, which, in spite of various protests, was every bit as good as concrete. So when the proprietors realised that the retreat was about to sound, they lost no time in switching camps and becoming zealous admirers of uproarious youth. They never failed to greet provocative remarks with a merry rejoinder, while Madame Jeannette bustled about in the café and Monsieur Louis stayed put behind the espresso machine and the beer tap. Maybe some evenings, fatigue playing its part, when they were cashing up, they might come out with an: Ah, the things we have to do, but as the long-haired students turned out to be just as hearty drinkers as the fishermen, although somewhat more boisterous, they looked forward to a comfortable old age when their troubles had come to an end.

The only thing they held against the long-haired tribe was that they were capable of spending a whole afternoon over just one drink, not thinking it necessary to repeat their order (and some of them used to put their heads through the door, see that all the seats were taken and turn on their heels, to the great displeasure of Madame Jeannette, who would run after them and assure them that she could always squeeze them in somewhere), or indulge in hectic games of table football, with returns, deciders, antithesis, synthesis, shouts, protests, after which Monsieur Louis and his lady eagerly encouraged the losers to stand a round.

Gyf, who to me was so far no more than an anonymous film maker, seemed to be an habitué of the place, which became apparent from the: The usual? Monsieur Louis sang out from behind his bar. The usual was a half of draught, which wasn't mine, but now that I had an admirer it was better not to risk upsetting him by making myself conspicuous and asking for tea, for instance, so when he asked me: That all right with you? I imprudently replied that that was all right with me. Imprudently, because at the fifth half, and after a few interruptions (excuse me, before disappearing through the door at the back; you had to ask for the key, which, far from annoying the proprietors, seemed to delight them, and each time I went past they showed their extreme consideration by suggesting they bring me the same again, so when I came back and sat down in front of a newly-filled glass I made a point of thanking Madame Jeannette, who was wiping the table after, probably in my excess of emotion, I had knocked the glass over, assuring me that it didn't matter, and, incidentally, another half for the gentleman, Louis), I began to wallow in self-pity. I was deeply moved that so many people should take an interest in me, it was too much for one day and, as always in such circumstances, the tears began to well up in my eyes. To Gyf, who showed concern at my too-visible emotion, I replied that it was nothing, it was just that I wasn't used to it. Would you rather have white wine? he asked.

So much thoughtfulness made it well worth my while to go along with the misunderstanding, which was why Gyf took it upon himself to order a bottle, which Madame Jeannette lost no time in bringing, with two little tumblers I immediately recognised: Duralex, Picardie model, 8cl (the smallest size – obviously in the interest of café proprietors), having sold hundreds of them in the shop and, ever since I was very young, accustomed to: Bonjour Madame, what may I do for you? – and the lady would say: Isn't your mother here? which is horribly vexing. As if when you're five or six you aren't perfectly capable of doing a sales pitch, of serving a customer who wants some drinking glasses, a useful clarification for anyone who is afraid he won't make himself understood, according to the principle: better too much than not enough, which is called laying it on with a trowel, which no one ever objects to in a man of the theatre, a film maker or a novelist, so why make fun of our purchasers? But in actual fact a drinking glass means an ordinary glass, an everyday one. The other sort, the elegant sort, the fragile sort on its single stem – they are put away in the cupboard, therefore you don't drink out of them, so you give the customer a choice of the different ordinary models, which anyway are all unbreakable, tempered glass, Madame, like my spectacles, just a simple matter of the way they're fired, but when it does shatter it's into a hundred billion pieces.

But this was not the moment to extol the merits of small shopkeeping. I kept my knowledge to myself and returned to our sheep shearing. Well, this film then, what does it actually talk about? abandoning all semantic precautions. The dialectician, his faculties somewhat blunted, wasn't so touchy now, and, having given it a moment's thought, and contemplated the row of bottles behind the bar, and shoved the lens of his spectacles further back into his eye-socket by pressing his finger on the frame at the top of his nose, suddenly confessed that actually it was him screwing a girlfriend. We had already made a good start on the bottle of white wine, my aesthetic ideas had become considerably broadened, and, having poured myself another glass which I downed in one gulp, too quickly no doubt because I suddenly had a fit of coughing and regurgitated a little liquid, I agreed that that was a really brilliant idea, and that I didn't understand why no one had ever thought of it before.

Very honestly, he contradicted me and said that it *had* already been thought of, that it was what was usually called porn, but – and he punctuated his remark with a gesture that swept away all confusion as well as his cigarette ash – they had nothing in common. Obviously not, what an idea, I wasn't the sort to confuse them. And what was there to see, actually? A guy and a doll, I don't need to explain, while he poured me another glass. No need, indeed, it couldn't be clearer. You'd really have to be a perverse revisionist to make any sort of comparison with the whoremasters of the cinema. So we saw the two of them, eh, that's to say you and? A girlfriend, he muttered evasively.

Excuse me. I must have stood up too precipitously because my chair fell over with a bang and managed to drag me down with it. While I was struggling to get back on to my feet Madame Jeannette came rushing up to the rescue, at the same time berating her husband: How often had she told him that that chair was rickety? No doubt about it, people were beginning to understand me better and better, life was beginning to seem less painful. Justice having been done, I got the key again. This time it was the lock that frustrated me. Someone must have messed about with it in the meantime, there was no way I could get the key into it, so after a few fruitless attempts I had the idea of reversing it and trying with the bow. This was when Monsieur Louis intervened, stating, following my remarks, that he had no intention of changing anything whatsoever, that it would do very well as it was until he retired, but, having opened the door for me, he added that I shouldn't hesitate to call him if I didn't feel well.

When I got back, another bottle was waiting for me, its neck still encircled by the white celluloid ring inscribed, in curiously gothic characters: Muscadet. A detail that was all the more significant in that Monsieur Louis, behind his counter, was entirely free to fill his bottles with whatever he chose, which, in the state we were in, was in any case perfectly acceptable. But, just at the sight of this further ordeal and of Gyf, crimson, slumped over the table, I suddenly felt sick and, without even taking time to excuse myself, rushed back to get the key, a chore which the diligent barman, no doubt fearing for the sawdust scattered all over his floor, wisely spared me, as with no further ado he flung the door wide open. I took advantage of these extra few seconds to return effortlessly and in the appropriate place a good proportion of what I had consumed. I feel better, I said to Gyf, who seemed worried to see me coming back looking so pale. And to fudge the issue, I added that the grub in the university restaurant wasn't always very fresh, that they gave us rotting meat, and that anyway I had already had an unfortunate experience of the sort at Saint-Cosmes, whereupon my friend cut me short, raised an eyelid – and this suddenly released a faint glimmer: Saint-Cosmes? I was there, in the first year.

Immediately, in spite of the fog – somewhat denser than usual – dancing in front of my eyes, the revelation: that lens stuck in his eye – who else could it be? Gyf, you're Gyf. And Gyf replied: No one has called me that for years. "What, then?" "Georges-Yves." But that's impossible, it's unpronounceable. No no, don't argue, for me and for all eternity you are Gyf, the unbelievable Gyf, the only person capable of going to the old nun on nursing duty, who usually just handed out aspirin, and telling her: Sister, my parts hurt. Parts of what? replies the old mustachioed nun, who knows as much about anatomy as she does about cooking, while two or three postulants for the infirmary are biting their cheeks to stop themselves falling about laughing. And the little guy with the asymmetrical glasses repeats, imperturbably: My parts, Sister. And Gyf said: Did I really do that? You certainly did, Gyf, how could I ever forget, we didn't so often get a chance to laugh, to revenge ourselves for the humiliations that rained down on us, what courage, what nerve, what imagination, but now I come to think of it: Your film, your film was already there, Mass had been said, by the time you were twelve you'd done it all, there was nothing to add. But Gyf played down this determinism: I was kindly not to tell him that after that he had screwed the old nun.

GYF UNCHANGED, GYF EXACTLY as he always was. But how had he managed to get through all those years alone, absolutely alone, because even more than his heroic exploits what impressed us was his solitude as a double orphan, his atrociously mutilated identity papers, and do you know that after they expelled you I too had a half-taste of that solitude? My father, who had taken me there and left me in the middle of the playground the day before the start of the school year at Saint-Cosmes – the boarders were already beginning to get down to work, and, from the very first evening in the dormitory, when all the lights were out and some of us, here and there, were choking back our tears with our heads in the bolster, young Gyf wrapped himself in a sheet and wandered around between the beds pretending to be a ghost, which, even before the school year had really begun, earned him his first session on his knees – the tall, white-haired man, who looked round for the last time before going back through the porch of the caretaker's lodge, maybe you remember – no though, why on earth should he remember? – and who waved to me one last time, well, the following year he left for good. Let me make myself clear: not for a new life, with another woman, for instance; he died, he died suddenly one day after Christmas, and do you know, I often thought of you? I told myself: You aren't the one that's most to be pitied: look at Gyf, he hasn't anyone at all and yet never a complaint, never a sob, and he's life itself.

Not entirely alone, he says, I had my grandmother. And it is perhaps the effect of the mixture of white wine and beer that causes a furtive, almost liquid mist to waft over the eyes of Gyf the Intrepid, and, as I am never at a loss when it comes to tears, I accompany him discretely, and drops of water are soon tumbling down into my white wine, but by the time I have rebuked myself for my sentimentality – stop thinking your tears show you to advantage, stop priding yourself on your rigidity – luckily Madame Jeannette, that subtle psychologist, has of her own accord brought another bottle (actually two thirty-three-centilitre half-bottles), and as I refill our tumblers I propose a toast to our reunion and to our future collaboration, because I now can't wait to see his film, I feel sure I'm going to like it.

Just imagine: a bed in the middle of a field, on the bed a couple making love, with all around them musicians playing and girls dancing topless with flowers in their hair. I could imagine it perfectly. A powerful, original work, a happening, but what really got to me was of a different order: what a lucky fellow Gyf was. How did he go about it, he with his glasses a hundred per cent reimbursed by the Social Security on account of being so unwearable, to get girls to undress so easily? Because after all, with that monocle-like lens that left a wrinkle under his eye when he took his specs off, that blob of a nose split like a chick-pea, that low forehead that gave the impression of having to indulge in a great deal of thought before coming up with an idea – what could the girls possible see in him? Not to mention that he probably washed his hair in engine oil. Did he dazzle them with promises of stardom? Was he playing at being a Hollywood producer, with the cigar replaced by roll-ups and sartorial elegance by cast-offs from the charity shop? Whereas I, during this time, being anxious to make a good impression, not wanting to make myself look too ridiculous with an abominable nylon thread round two lenses as thick as the bottom of this bottle, *I* moved about in a haze, and deprived myself of the sight of the beauties of this world solely to avoid reading in their eyes the scorn they felt at the lamentable figure I cut. Perhaps, if I followed in his wake, I might enter the kingdom of naked girls? What did he want from me, then? If he was thinking of making a sequel, I could always suggest he put another bed in the field, for example.

More bothered than I thought possible by this innovative kind of film making, I began to disparage my Jean-Arthur and all my literary pretensions: what's the point of accumulating words and phrases so laboriously, of wresting them from the blankness of the page, what's the use of all that time spent, wasted, in searching for the right setting and the right words? Gyf, shall I tell you? – *you're* the one who's got it right. I have a terrible urge to drop out of the arts faculty and have a go at scriptwriting. It doesn't seem all that complicated, and then it rather looks as if you get more involved, as if you put more of yourself into it. Actually, your girlfriend. Which one? The one, I mean, in bed with you, in the middle of the field.

My grandmother, says Gyf, becoming emotional again. The field belonged to my grandmother, she left it to me when she died, with a little house, in Logrée, you know Logrée? No, but your girlfriend. It's on the banks of the Loire. Yes, I can imagine it, or at least more or less, but that girl, the star in your film? For me, there aren't any stars, no roles more important than any others; and anyway there aren't any roles. Well of course not, I know that, I was only teasing, but that girl, in the bed, who with, isn't her name Yvette? No, why? do you know her? Gyf enquires anxiously, and, possibly afraid that he has put his foot in it or that there is some sort of amorous imbroglio, painfully raises an eyelid and for the nth time, tapping his finger on his cigarette, aims wide of the ashtray and drops a cylinder of ash which dissolves in a pool of white wine. No no, I don't know her, it was just that in that case the title of your film would have been ready-made. How come? Obviously, listen: Gyf sur Yvette.

Lowering his eyelids, he managed a compassionate little smile, just enough to show me that in spite of his state he had caught the subtlety of my play on words but didn't hold it against me, and that was even more terrible than if he had requested me to mind my own business. With that little smile, all my dreams of the cinema collapsed, which was much the same as saying all my dreams of being rescued from my solitude. I was a little fed up with myself because I knew, in the same way as I reproached myself for my propensity to tears, that I always did better when I kept my mouth shut, but how could I not let myself become intoxicated by that sudden exaltation, that unexpected breath of youth? I didn't have so many opportunities to become a stowaway on one of these fashionable bandwagons. How can you not dream of being different from what you are, when the horizon is dark and everyday life is unattractive? The awakening was, as was to be expected, brutal, and it was only right that I should get sent back to my cell and my literary labours, to my Jean-Arthur or something of the sort, that's to say to the same old life, to my three eternally-repeated chords, and to scraping away at my sheep, as if, after I had believed that

I had finally escaped from it, the circle of sadness and boredom had once again closed around me.

Everything was returning to normal. And anyway, Gyf explained that I had nothing to regret, because even if his girlfriend *had* been called Yvette, in the scene that seemed to worry me (I didn't even bother to protest), she wasn't underneath, but on top. And then, it already had a title. Really? – what is it? Once again Gyf became solemn, and, blowing his cigarette smoke up to the yellowed ceiling, told me, almost shyly: *A Tomb for Grandmother*.

That's very beautiful, Gyf.

I WAS CERTAINLY BECOMING VERY much in demand. For the second time in two days someone knocked on my door. No doubt I could even have deduced that this someone was anxious for my company, given the insistence with which he was drumming. And this inappropriate hammering almost made me regret my previous solitude. In the ordinary way, at least in the ordinary way in the movies, which is inevitably somewhat perfunctory, such a deployment of energy lends itself to a dual interpretation: it's either to warn the occupier that there's a fire and to encourage a precipitate evacuation of the building, or to make sure he hasn't croaked, in which case – still in the movies – they break the door down.

The idea of roasting was not incompatible with a radical treatment for my headache. Anything would be preferable to this sensation of an anti-personnel mine lurking at the root of every hair, as if my skull had been turned into a bunker and was being used as a site for experiments with a new range of explosives, but the prospect of the problems suggested by the second hypothesis – a door broken down (tell the concierge, explain myself, call a carpenter, pay the bill) – forced me to a desperate manoeuvre: to try to get up.

Immediately, once I had employed my remaining traces of thought in calling myself every name under the sun and my conduct of the previous evening unspeakable,

I realised that every somewhat abrupt movement was to be banished, if only in order to avoid any automatic reaction that might cause the disintegration of my gelatinous cerebral matter, which seemed to be immersed in a vinous magma like a cockleshell swept away by a demented sea. No sooner had I set foot on land than it became apparent: one; that I had slept fully dressed and with my shoes on, which was not among my habits, two; that my shoes were reposing in a sort of pumpkin soup, which had inconsiderately spread over those few pages of my Jean-Arthur still lying on the floor and were here and there covered with unidentifiable lumps which, except for some sinuous little white worms that I more or less identified as bits of spaghetti, I found it difficult to reconstitute into my previous day's meal, and three; that the floor, the ceiling and the walls began to dance a frantic jig the moment I tried to bring the facts of my present situation to light by attempting, without causing too much damage, to raise two leaden eyelids.

Gyf, to whom I opened the door, didn't ask me how things were, which is to say that the moment he caught sight of me he said he wouldn't ask me how things were. He even let out a little whistle when he discovered the state of my room, after which he made a brief comment, something about being half seas over, but to me that immediately conjured up the demented sea and the raging tempest furiously beating against the dome of my skull. He, though, seemed to be in fairly good shape, with his hair slicked down as usual and the permanent stubble on his face, but I had to make do with this first impression, finding it very hard to keep my eyes open on account of the instability of the walls. He then reminded me that there were showers at the end of the corridor on this floor, and strongly advised me to make the most of them. We'll wait for you, he said, so I blindly grabbed a few toilet articles and a random change of clothes, and mumbled: We're on our way, showing by this echo a form of wit which, in the circumstances, reassured me: my vital organs didn't seem to be affected.

When we came back, our hair dripping, having managed to defuse a few mines, a fairy godmother had been at work on my pathetic dwelling. The floor, with its big black and white tiles, was shining, which could have made me think that as a victim of a hallucinogenic Muscadet I had been in the grip of a sporadic derangement of the senses. Then I suddenly began to worry about my pumpkin pages. There certainly had been some on the floor, I remembered that perfectly, what with my habit of leaving everything lying around, there was a long mono-logue, in which my Jean-Arthur described how he danced to the rhythm of a tomtom after he had negotiated an arms deal with a negro king, which had cost me a lot of hard work, hours of dogged perseverance sounding out the syllables, choosing them for their rhythmic potential, at the same time doing my best to reproduce the local colour, the red earth and the songs of the natives, the thatched huts and the paraphernalia of the sorcerer, the movement of the bodies in a state of trance and the swaying of the women's breasts – and this last image brought me back to Gyf's film. Gyf, however, assured me that he hadn't done a thing, I should ask Theo. Theo – who was that? That's me, she said.

I couldn't bear anyone messing about with my papers. It always made me nervous to think that anybody might so much as cast an eye on a phrase, a handful of words, which, out of context and manipulated by an ill-intentioned individual, ran the risk of being ridiculed. And their author, at the same time. What put a stop to my bad-tempered reaction was that Theo, then, whom I discovered at the same time as she showed me my yellowish manuscript spread out on the desk, Theo who had played Cinderella by mopping up a good part of the reserve stock of the *Au Bon Pêcheur,* Theo who had that odd nickname which I would have to elucidate one day, Theo who had arrived at the same time as this mystery (but how was it that Gyf, decked out in such dreadful glasses, attracted such pretty girls?), Theo who had stayed in the corridor at first and seen me groping my way along it with my eyes closed and my hand on the wall, Theo, since it was she – Theo had a disarming smile. And that was what it must have been, because, after she had quoted a couple of phrases from my Jean-Arthur, instead of automatically excusing myself, instead of mumbling that it was only a draft, of trying to convince her that I was capable of much better things, I declared – and as I heard myself doing so I both cursed and blessed the peyotl-laced Muscadet of Monsieur Louis and Madame Jeannette – that I would really like to have been the author of such phrases. They were rather well turned, weren't they? And do you know what? She agreed with me.

After that there was a moment – a very short one, but even so, a moment – when I felt I was finally approaching my goal. Life was not so uncomfortable for someone who found his place in it. In short, life was playable. And this feeling had nothing to do with any secret triumph, with taking my revenge on fate, it was simply a question of common sense; things were finally taking their normal course. But very soon, in spite of the state I was in, I came back to my senses. It was all much too obvious. I wasn't born yesterday. Seeing that their previous methods had failed (I hadn't cracked up when I heard that the love of my youth had drowned, nor had I talked under the influence of drink), they were now trying to get at me through my feelings, counting on my sense of frustration by pretending to be interested in my Jean-Arthur. I recognised this as being in the great classic line of espionage. And anyway, Theo smacked of a code name. Yet her difference from the previous agents was considerable. Or rather, it was a difference of nature. Of type, in short, and that's what this one absolutely was – my type.

And after all, I was beginning to weary of the struggle, my Jean-Arthur was more and more complaining of his solitude, you could no longer rely on the stability of walls, and I simply couldn't face the idea of once again taking to the maquis of my inner resistance to an imaginary invader. The time for surrender was at hand. That disarming smile, whose mechanism I was gradually beginning to perceive: a sulky upper lip, brilliant-black eyes, and a little beauty spot on her cheekbone which moved up towards her eye when her smile became more pronounced – that smile which had been miraculously parachuted into my field of vision by a mysterious revenant, nothing could be sadder than the thought that crossed my befuddled mind that I might soon see it fade, recede, disappear maybe for ever from my perimeter of clarity and melt into the great terrestrial haze, carried away by the beautiful student with the wavy brown hair bunched behind her neck in a red ribbon, standing in the middle of my room, her hands in the pockets of a hooded, frogged *kabig,* the Breton duffel coat which was perfectly in keeping with the tone of the place (I myself, like a good third of the faculty, was wearing a navy blue reefer jacket), apart from its colour: duck-egg blue.

That personal touch, that duck-egg blue, which made such an elegant contrast to the navy blues and khakis, *that* anyway was proof that with rare beings rarity is everywhere, and so: Gyf! – why did you have to bring me that particular smile? Which is so rare that I haven't much chance of coming across it at every street corner – not that I've ever noticed people smiling at each other at street corners. This ephemeral apparition in the life of a copyist monk that I lead will only revive my regrets. May I add that I can imagine that the day will come when, in a conceivable moment of depression, I shall miss that smile terribly.

All the more so in that the beauty seemed to be very well informed about my literary activities. And she wanted to know how far I had got, whether I thought I would soon finish it, whether I wasn't tempted to incorporate extracts from other texts into my text (yes, I know, women like to look after these savage invalids on their return from tropical climes). In fact, as I showed my astonishment – because how, in two phrases, had she guessed everything? – it came out that, don't you remember? – we had already discussed these questions the previous evening. Now you're having me on. Gyf, she's having me on. She's taking advantage of the state I'm in. That's how people drive other people mad, they get them to believe that they've . . . they sow doubt, and afterwards . . . You're the one who's having us on, said Gyf. Me? Yes, don't tell me . . . Don't tell you what? Talk about being half seas over, Gyf repeated.

And the little beauty spot moves up towards the corner of her eye again, while I envisage the worst – and I am so overcome with shame that I forget the anti-personnel mines and dancing walls and am getting ready to blush with embarrassment and add yet another chapter to the big book of my humiliations. That was as far as I had got, let's think, my mind's a maelstrom, no, Gyf, don't prompt me, ah yes, at the *Tomb for Grandmother* in the café with Madame Jeannette and Monsieur Louis. It's true that after that there's what they call a gap in my memory; however hard I search, dig, rack my brains, I can't manage to make the connection between that last moment and the moment when the drum beats sounding the reveille on my door woke me up, which actually also implies a gap in my timetable. And when I say gap, it's actually very much like a passage through the shadows. And yet it would seem that I was with you. And, without going into detail, what did we do?

Nothing special. That reassured me a little. But then what? Among other things, we went on drinking. Hence those rumblings at the roots of my hair. And the spaghetti-based regurgitation pellets? After that we joined Theo and some friends and all went back with one of them to his place for what was suppposed to be an Italian evening, or rather let's call it a pasta-based evening. And personally, without necessarily wishing to see everything in terms of myself, how did I behave? Somewhat later, I had fallen asleep. And before I sank into a coma? No inappropriate declarations, no incongruous or even improper behaviour to report? No, not really, except that you kept insisting almost obsessively that you wanted to kiss Theo.

Ah. So there we are. The capillary rumblings become increasingly demented, and several anti-personnel mines have just exploded simultaneously. I find it extremely difficult to raise my head, and my whole face has suddenly become as hot as if the blazing sun is beating down on me. And yet I had to meet the gaze of the beautiful

Theo, find the courage to apologise profusely, and at least promise not to do it again, even though I had already given up all hope of there being any future occasions. She could insist on my making amends, anything she liked, but whatever happened nothing could eradicate my feeling of shame or, to be more precise – because after all it isn't particularly gratifying – my feeling of profound malediction, which is to say: who, if he were me, could bear to be me? She should understand that I wouldn't wish that on anyone, unless perhaps my worst enemy – for *him* to make himself look ridiculous in everyone's eyes wouldn't necessarily be a bad thing – , but honestly, people ought to stop holding it against me. Or else, just you have a try at being me, in which case I wish you joy. (Although you might possibly get some from my Jean-Arthur, because it'll be up to you to finish it – but to be honest I would rather do it myself, as I have a few very precise ideas about its style and lyricism, and personally I trust my ear, which in this hypothesis would be yours of course, but let's imagine a change of eardrums in the course of the transfer, and then what would become of my beautiful text? There is too great a risk that it would become distorted, so even if it means putting up with myself a bit longer I think – although I have my doubts – I *think* I prefer to remain myself, to carry on, and put my name to my story.)

My cheeks were burning with shame, but that was nothing in comparison with the question that was burning my lips: if Theo had chosen to visit the condemned man in his cell, was it in order to light the fire under the stake and watch the author of the crime slowly roast to death, or – and naturally such a thought was accompanied by the most extreme reservations – had she come to make sure of the power of her charms over the said victim now undergoing his detoxication phase? In which case there was no need for her to worry, I was just as overcome by emotion as if she was appearing to me for the first time. I perfectly understood that I had fallen in love with her at first sight and that I had gone so far – with the aid of the liberating effect of the wine – as to give a little rein to my feelings. I simply regretted not having kept the memory of the savour of her lips – always supposing that she had allowed herself to be kissed by me. Which was doubtful, considering that as I understood it we had ended up at her boyfriend's place, and he had not appreciated the further fact that after ingestion, I had poured back two or three glasses of wine on to his bedspread.

But she was there, and there without her hygiene maniac. If you believe her, she had come to find out how I was, having been afraid that I might never wake up and that my alcoholic coma might last longer than a night's healing sleep. She was glad to see me in more or less good condition, and hoped that it would soon be sufficiently improved for me to be able to tell her about my writings, whose excellence and innovative character I had been vaunting the previous evening.

This latest news was greeted by a new salvo of anti-personnel mines, so I took advantage of the tumult generated by their detonation to stammer – without forcing my voice to the point of risking hearing myself – two or three sheepish words about my scandalous conduct the previous evening. As for my writing, obviously she shouldn't believe everything I might have told her – of which I hadn't the slightest recollection, even if I had happened to pronounce judgments which alternated between the enthusiastic and the depressed – about the reality of my presumed talents. As the barometer of my feelings, if I could believe what she said, had come to rest on Set Fair, it would be logical for her to observe that this morning – oh really, it was after noon? – the weather had considerably worsened, that the anticyclone had been followed by a deep depression, and that therefore, if she would be kind enough to do me this favour, we would speak about it at some other time. This strategy of the carrot also allowed me the hope of seeing her again soon.

Gyf, though, had another idea. We had a Minister for the Armed Forces, or for War, or for Revenge, who had judged it opportune to mobilise all young people, and therefore all students, in view of a planetary conflict whose imminence had so far escaped us. Hence, certainly out of ignorance, a kind of reluctance greeted the measure announced.

Up to the present, a young man had been allowed to ask for his military service to be postponed until after he had completed his studies, and if this respite was granted it was called deferment. But, perhaps fearing that a considerable prolongation of studies might eventually lead to an army of more or less old men who would be only moderately inclined to make a gift of their bodies to the motherland (and we know that organs that have had their day are no longer any use), we were invited to do our national duty with no further delay, as the army has always been nourished by young, ardent blood. When we got to the right age, we would leave as a matter of urgency to serve our country. There would be plenty of time to resume our studies when we got back.

Can you imagine? Just when you are finally about to learn what E is equal to, you are called to the colours. Where you count one-two, one-two, which seems to be fundamental to the act of marching or even walking (even though babies can walk before they can count), you learn that a barrack-room mate has removed the top of a bottle of beer with his teeth, you accumulate an incalculable number of funny stories with which you mean to regale your friends the moment you are returned to civilian life, you go out in a group in which, as if you weren't already conspicuous enough what with your orthopaedic boots, your unbecoming uniform and your crew cut, you make yourself even more conspicuous by kicking dustbins, you improve your repertory of more or less refined songs which, on leave, you sing in trains, sprawling in the corridors and even in the passages between the coaches, and, when the great day finally arrives, the day of your liberation, you bawl at the top of your voice: *Quille bordel*! and hoist up a ninepin as far as your arm can reach. Which has the effect of thoroughly bemusing any foreign tourist who has the misfortune to be travelling with you. He may quite likely know that a *quille* is a ninepin, and he'll have a good idea of what a bordel is. But: Ninepin brothel? So you kindly inform him that quille is army slang for demob, and that bordel is one of those lexical items their dictionaries warn them may have certain additional vulgar meanings. (However, ninepins now being exclusively manufactured for the purpose of this particular rite, it just goes to show that it isn't only the armaments industry that benefits from military service.) You do all this without realising the extent to which you have lost contact with the civilised world, so once you are back in the lecture room and someone who has no idea of the enormous amount of knowledge you have accumulated in just one year suddenly pounces on you and asks: Well then, E is equal to what?, taken by surprise, searching your memory after that sabbatical interruption, you hazard: Two right angles? And you copy out three hundred billion times – but just for yourself, because at that level the only punishment you are given is to be referred to your sense of responsibility – and you ask yourself: But what the devil was I doing with that crew?

For Gyf and a few others, who had already begun to organise the resistance, such a challenge to the status quo of the deferment rule was not negotiable. Therefore the forces of obscurantism must be made to retreat by mass actions which would encompass the entire range of our brothers, the toiling classes. Even though this had caused Gyf some disappointment when he was distributing tracts at dawn at the gates of the Batignolles factories. The jeers of our comrades who couldn't care less about the reform (the younger men had more of a tendency to enlist before they were called up) had reassured him about the persistence of the proletarian spirit, but he was not so pleased when the employers' perfidious militia, represented by three or four couples of hatchet men, had unceremoniously sent him back to his studies.

This incident was responsible for him acquiring a new pair of glasses, even more rustic than the previous ones (which had shattered on contact with the paving stones), a way, according to him, of getting even closer to the world of the exploited, although they, at the same time, were saving up in order to acquire more elegant frames. And this, this aspiration to be better looking, worried Gyf so much that he got to the point of wondering whether he wouldn't do better next time – but let's get this straight: only so as not to lose contact with the oppressed masses, even if he had to espouse their petit-bourgeois desires – to choose a more attractive design. At any rate he intended to raise the problem at the next meeting of the cell he had himself created, following a split with the tiny group of the Monguist persuasion on account of a profound disagreement on the question of the make up of female militants. Of *what* persuasion, Gyf? He pushed his glasses right up into his eye. Don't tell me you don't know Mong?

In the ordinary way, in such circumstances I would resign myself to answering: But of course I do, although only too well aware of the disastrous consequences and the backlash a lying assertion would entail, but fortunately Theo declared that she had never heard of him. Nor have I, I said, relieved and happy to share my ignorance with the beauty.

Mong was a peasant in the Kingdom of Siam who, in the twelfth century, had organised an armed struggle against a feudal lord whose dogs had devoured his meagre herds. But, after the vote by show of hands had concluded that Mong would have been opposed to female militants making themselves up, Gyf had taxed him with archaeo-conservatism, and since then had been carefully studying the history of the village of la Brière in search of a vernacular model who, in his view, would be more likely to revitalise regional revolutionary fervour. He had just discovered a certain Aoustin, who in the seventeenth century had had a brush with the excisemen, not on account of salt smuggling (the salt-producing region being on his doorstep) but following a quarrel over a woman, which had led to a peasants' revolt that had been savagely suppressed. The Gyfian faction was on the point of announcing its birth to the world of the outcasts, there were just a few finishing touches to be put to the rules, particularly in the matter of the distribution of ministries between the Monguists and the Aoustinians (both movements acknowledging that without the other they were not strong enough to hope to seize power). But in the meantime they had to get a move on: the General Meeting, which was to debate the wording of the rallying cries for the demonstration planned for that afternoon, was about to begin.

The lecture hall was packed. Some students had taken refuge on the window sills and a few girls had climbed up on to the shoulders of sturdy male colleagues, where they were playing at being semaphorists, from time to time waving at a friend they had spotted. It was not only the seats that were occupied but all the desks as well. Gyf pushed his way through the bodies blocking the steps towards a handful of Monguist militants he had recognised at the foot of the platform, where three hirsute young men were officiating, taking turns at the mike to preside over the debate. Above the young assembly floated a stagnant cloud of smoke, becoming denser by the moment. On the benches, the cigarette rollers were working flat out, the more sensitive among them leaving the job of licking the gummed paper to their sleeping partners. But it was a veritable industry, with composite effluvia. The more impecunious took turns at solemnly savouring deep, sensuous, precious drags on the same blackened fag end, inhaling at length and with religious fervour, thus resembling conscientious seekers after health, after which they discharged a delicate cone of haze into the atmosphere with the ecstatic look of someone who has successfully performed a ritual.

Theo didn't seem in any hurry to join Gyf. Responding to the wave of a great big curly-haired antipathetic blond by a gracious little gesture, she whispered a few banal words in my ear, which, judging by the way he turned his head and suddenly became interested in the debate, the antipathetic individual no doubt interpreted as a disparaging remark about him. I guessed that he was imagining all sorts of things about my relationship with the beauty in the duck-egg-blue kabig, which gladdened my heart and, if it had been possible to stop the march of the universe at that moment, I would have asked nothing else from life than the infinite repetition of this pure, jewel-like instant which illuminated my ravaged spirit. I merely privately deplored the fact that this antipathetic character had too much imagination.

The atmosphere was genuinely fraternal; calling everyone *tu* was obligatory. The whole idea of hierarchy had been abolished, everyone was invited to say what he thought, and even the mandarin who had strayed into the meeting and who stood up in the middle of catcalls to express a reactionary opinion was sharply snubbed with a: Shut up, Comrade, you'll get a chance to speak when it's your turn. The comrade professor, who was within a couple of years of retirement, protested, demanding in the first place to be addressed as *vous*, and was immediately taxed with being a reactionary bastard. The constituent assembly applauded knowledgeably, and came to the unanimous conclusion that he had really asked for it.

And now they were approaching the tricky stage of the operation. Everyone was agreed on the basics: the ministerial measure was iniquitous and tended to exclude the children of the working classes from extended studies. What was the likelihood of the son of a peasant or a prole-tarian returning to higher education after a gap of over a year? There was a brief skirmish between the advocates of zero per cent and those who counted on a successful indoctrination of the labouring classes resulting in a salu-tary awakening, and who didn't despair of some sort of a percentage being attained. A compromise motion was arrived at, although it didn't leave much hope for our underprivileged comrades. An unmade-up female militant proposed that the measure should be accepted in exchange for the creation of genuinely popular universities where everybody, from cleaning women to dustmen, would be able to study free, at all ages and without any previous qualifications: some, jam-making; some, Spinoza's ethics; some, the theory of relativity; some, macramé; some, Euclid's thirty-second theorem. This was interesting, of course, but a comrade mathematician pointed out that you learnt Euclid's thirty-second theorem before you even went to secondary school so he didn't see the need for a university, even a popular one, to teach it. As for jam, he would be glad to give the militant girl his grandmother's recipes. Boo! boo! went the assembly. Silence, comrades. A vote was taken: the proposition was rejected. That was when Gyf was seen going up to the unmade-up militant, probably a Monguist, apparently in an attempt to convert her to the Aoustinians.

Now it was time to pass on to serious matters. This, at least, was the opinion of one of the chairmen of the debate. A lapse of concentration on his part, a moment of fatigue, maybe. Because to talk of what was to follow as serious matters, implied that everything that had so far been said was not serious. That was a procedure worthy of the Stalinist trials, someone protested. Good point – except that the person who had made it found himself immediately reproached for deliberately and shamelessly trying to confuse the dictatorship of the proletariat with the totalitarianism of any old banana republic. Objection sustained – and a vote by show of hands was then taken to decide who should replace Comrade Roger Lanzac (not, of course, the celebrated presenter of the celebrated *Piste aux*

Etoiles that we used to watch at Uncle Rémi's in the days when he was one of the rare people in the village to own a television set), but this gibe was enough to destabilise the chairman, who immediately launched into his self-criticism. And our Gyf was elected to take his place. Theo and I were very proud. I took advantage of this to move a little closer to her, to smile at her, and to make the odd comment. I was caught up in the great revolutionary wave, I glimpsed a radiant future, somewhere between the heavenly Jerusalem and the kingdom of the angels.

As the advertised march was just about to start, Gyf wasted no time in tackling the fundamental question of the slogans. After summing up the situation he took a rapid sounding of the audience, from which it became apparent that the most frequently-occurring rallying cry was: No to the Army. This was sober, meaningful, and spoke for itself. People were already beginning to stand up when Gyf once again grabbed the mike and announced in dramatic tones: Comrades, at one stroke you have just condemned the struggle of the oppressed peoples trying to throw off the imperialist yoke. What was that? What was he on about? We were whole-heartedly pro the oppressed peoples. Every oppressed people was welcome. It was almost as if we couldn't find enough of them, the strength of our indignation was so inexhaustible. We dreamed of adopting some of them. How fortunate was the lucky fellow who, taking advantage of a formidable connection with someone in the right place – an uncle who was a missionary, for example – could go to work as the representative of a tribe from the Matto Grosso which was under threat from a powerful multinational company, and whose survival depended only on our signature at the bottom of a roneotyped tract. We really could not allow ourselves to be suspected of collusion with the clique of liberticidal, starvation-wage-paying employers. Gyf was exaggerating, but he went even further: You are playing the game of all the paper tigers, of all the papier-mâché lions. What would become of our Vietnamese brothers – and sisters, prompted the unmade-up militant – and sisters, Gyf added, anxious to swell the ranks of the Aoustinians – if, by condemning all armies, you oppose the creation of a popular liberation force, the only thing capable of breaking the neo-colonialist chains that subjugate the peoples in the sole interest of profit. Long live the proletarian army, yelled Gyf. Long live the army of the people. The audience – at least those who had found their places – sat down again. The point raised by our comrade friend warranted discussion. In the first place, the aggressor had to be clearly identified. That was easy enough: The Americans and their stooges. Just a minute though, Gyf warned. America also produces its exploited, with whom we are in complete solidarity, and he added a few words in favour of our red brothers – and sisters – and sisters who were organising their resistance on the very same soil that nourished in its bosom the degenerate, bloodthirsty offspring of post slave-trading capitalism. For who was at the source of all wars? The guilty party, they knew as well as he did, was always, everywhere, the same. So just one rallying cry: No to the Army of Capitalism, Gyf yelled into the mike.

It had to be acknowledged that our friend's mastery of dialectics had considerably advanced the discussion. It only remained to put the finishing touches to the concept, so after the tabling of a series of amendments followed by a vote by show of hands, the following slogan was unanimously adopted: No to the Army of Capitalism,

Yes to the Popular Army of Liberation of our brothers –
and sisters – in their fight against Imperialism. Which had
a really great ring to it. But actually it was not quite unanimous. When all the hands had been lowered, one got
raised again, and proceeded to take the floor (or rather,
its owner did). While manifesting his solidarity with all
exploited people and without denying the necessity of
pursuing the struggle by their side, he was nevertheless
worried that no one had mentioned the subject which,
after all, was the reason for our presence here: the challenge to the deferment rule. And it so happened that, as
the son of a peasant, he was particularly vulnerable to
this legal measure because he had already had a great deal
of trouble in persuading his family to allow him to go
to university. There was absolutely no doubt that after
a year in the army the question would not even have
arisen. A profound silence fell over the assembly, followed
by a murmur which would have been frankly disapproving
had he been the son of a shopkeeper. Gyf considered the
comrade peasant's remark interesting, but time was up,
the meeting had already gone on too long, and he asked us
to meet outside the prefecture of police.

A COLD, FINE, DRIZZLE WAS falling as we marched. The sky was in its grey wintry mood where there is no blue break in the clouds to be expected, no bright spell to hope for, nothing for it but to accept the hibernal darkness the way you accept love or death. The demonstration advanced slowly, brows knitted, parkas tightly done up, in the meagre, leaden light which already heralded a premature end to the afternoon. Gyf, who had taken his glasses off on account of the rain, was in one of the first rows but behind the official leaders, who had only moderately appreciated his speech, and were perhaps afraid that this day might be the prelude to a reversal of fortunes in favour of the Aoustinians and their charismatic chief, in spite of his peculiar glasses. They clung on to their loudspeaker, refusing to let go of it and obstinately shouting out their own slogans, which were much too complicated and therefore didn't meet with any great enthusiasm from the marchers. The latter, giving feeble voice just to warm themselves up, had anyway very soon adopted the prosaic: Down with the Army, which corresponded much more closely with their immediate preoccupations. But the whole thing was very lacklustre, seemed very amateur, and, not to put too fine a point on it, a bit constipated. This obvious lack of conviction hadn't escaped a group of would-be blithe spirits, who had got it into their heads that it was up to them to give the demonstration a bit of a boost, to restore it to its festive, undergraduate vocation, and were playing the clown, shouting bawdy remarks at the passers-by and generally making us feel ashamed of them.

Demonstrating is an art. It isn't enough just to march behind the banners and join in the chorus of the songs with revamped words that a militant poet is bawling through his megaphone shaped like a flower complete with its central pistil (for example, when someone is demanding a rise from a boss whose name is Pierre, you get: Au clair de la lune, mon ami Pierrot, you'll soon change your tune, if we aren't paid more dough). And you have to look totally convinced, almost fierce, but at the same time still good-natured, a bit of a joker but prudish, a bon vivant but with good manners, in order to prove that a militant doesn't spurn the fruits of his labours but is careful not to over-indulge in them and is therefore both serious and lighthearted, all the time advancing with a slow step without giving the impression that you are dragging your feet, remembering to aim understanding smiles at the passers-by massed on the edge of the pavement, refusing to engage in polemics with the agitators who call you layabouts, and above all giving the impression that nothing on earth could make you want to be anywhere else.

Behind the hard core of fanatics leading the march the rows very soon began to thin out, as if, by keeping his distance behind his comrades, everyone was doing his best to put in an appearance without really seeming to be there, lowering his head, stopping in front of a shop window, casually taking up a slogan with an air of being surprised at having said something, hugging the pavements in the hope of being taken for one of the customers, moving away from a troublemaker with the air of Saint Peter swearing he doesn't know this man, scrupulously doing the sort of minimum duty necessary to remain within the ambient spirit of revolt.

Theo, the gentle rebel, was walking slowly, in silence, her hands in her pockets, her wide, Capuchin friar's hood pulled down so far that in profile you couldn't even see the tip of her nose, just the little cloud of condensed breath that came out of her mouth when, now and then emerging from her shelter and stretching her neck, she made a remark about the weather not looking as if it was going to get any better. And in fact it didn't get any better, the rain was falling harder and faster and now forming puddles on the road, thus obliging us to take little dance steps to avoid them, a good excuse to break the monotony of the march.

This association of water and dancing reminded me of my drowned naiad, and I sneaked a look at Theo's black slippers which made an elegant contrast with the army of trainers, ankle boots, clogs with leather straps, galoshes, and even – a Spartan no doubt – flipflops. When Theo made a gracious little jump over a puddle I felt brave enough to ask her whether she had ever gone in for ballet, and at the same time whether she liked swimming. I saw a mischievous eye emerge from under her hood, and without waiting for an answer succumbed to despair at having once again gratuitously put myself in the wrong. (Would a father – *my* father, all things considered – have taught me the art of keeping my mouth shut, or at least of talking advisedly, always finding the right, witty, sensitive, precise word? If so, his premature death had caused me to lose a great deal . . .) So I hastened to add that this was because of the rain, now really pelting down, which, if you didn't know the sub-text, was a pretty feeble remark. Whereupon, torn between the likelihood of getting thoroughly soaked at any moment and the certainty of looking totally ridiculous, I settled for the second solution and took out of the pocket of my reefer jacket a khaki-coloured cloth cap which I had surreptitiously bought at an American surplus shop, and this, dropping back a step or two, hoping the beauty wouldn't notice, I cautiously put on as best I could (not all the anti-personnel mines had exploded), checking in the mirror of a car parked on the pavement that the peak was at the right angle. Then, quickening my steps, I caught up with my blue Capuchin nun.

Who had stopped, and was waiting for me, observing my little manoeuvre from inside her hood. Decidedly, no matter what efforts one makes to escape one's condition they are rarely crowned with success. Theo suddenly bursts out laughing, which of course is enough to intimidate you, so, not knowing what sort of a face to put on it, you meet it with a contrite, resigned little smile, because for that particular laugh you are prepared to accept every vexation, every wound to your amour-propre, and the reason for this is simple: in the heart of your solitude, in the midst of the undulations of the waves, night after night, full of despair yet full of hope, you fabricated a tender dream that resembles her. You take it upon yourself to explain it to her, but, rather like when you're staging your own death, you get somewhat tangled up in the medico-scientific arguments you have read in a magazine and tried to put into practice: something to the effect that heat loss occurs essentially through the head, and therefore if you don't want your feet to get cold, which is the most painful of all, you had better wear something on your head, otherwise it's like heating a house that doesn't have a roof, or like sleeping in the open air, and from there you go on to the infinite spaces: Pluto, a planet that is too far away because the sun's rays are too short to reach it, ice on Mars, intergalactic chill ... but, cutting short your exposition on supernovae, white dwarfs, red giants or whatever, the beauty decides that the moment has come to take leave of the demonstration.

What about Gyf? I pleaded. Who are you talking about? Georges-Yves I mean, I said, articulating as if I was trying to say she sells seashells on the seashore, Gyf – that was in the old days, at school. Oh, he was nowhere near finished, between now and tomorrow he would certainly hold half a dozen more meetings to discuss a hundred thousand fascinating things about the future of humanity, in particular whether Mong or Aoustin would have been the first to walk on the Moon. But, if I had no objection to changing the subject – goodness, she wasn't all that fascinated by Gyf – she thought it might be a good idea to find somewhere nice and warm to sit in front of something restorative. At which point, instead of looking back to check all around me whether her remark was not addressed to someone else (although I am not a complete idiot, and I did actually realise, however bizarre it might seem, that she meant me), I took the initiative and, when the procession turned a corner, I carried straight on in the direction of a little café with misted-up windows, with the beauty at my side. This escapade, this manner of giving someone the slip, you can well imagine, my place ... not for anything in the world ...

The moment she sat down Theo tossed her hood back and it was like a little miracle, the revelation of her face seen from so close to, barely the width of the table, that's to say the only distance, about fifty centimetres, at which I could see clearly. Her domed forehead was unencumbered by her nearly-black hair, which was loosely tied behind her neck in a red ribbon. Her black eyes sparkled, but it was an interior sparkle, and you didn't have to be a great genius to read the rather forced message behind it which her eyes were sending you. Her insistence on keeping them screwed up when she smiled almost ended by making her smile seem painful, even though, as she later admitted, the way she screwed them up was partly due to the effort she made to counter her slight myopia, which in the long run gave her such violent headaches that she had no option but to wear glasses at lectures (whereupon I told her that there was a far simpler solution: Just don't try to see). And then her unplucked eyebrows, contrary to the prevailing fashion, the slightly rounded tip of her nose, the tiny beauty spot like a dark spot of dust that had settled on her cheekbone and which you wanted to flick off, her sulky upper lip, and her chin that turned her face into an oval . . . but the waiter was already there, holding his tray up at shoulder level, waiting for our order – or rather for Theo's order, actually – simpering as he stared at her, merely granting me a rapid, haughty glance – huh, a casting error – Theo was giving it some thought while unbuttoning her kabig (light-coloured oblong wooden buttons which in the old days were also used as whistles, but I wasn't going to ask her to try to blow them), revealing a black mohair pullover and a long slender neck. But since black has a tendency to blur human forms, as it had for my drowned girl, I didn't feel like lowering my eyes.

All the time Theo was making up her mind, the man in the waistcoat didn't seem to be in a hurry, but now that she had made her choice he practically forced me to decide on the first thing that came to mind – the same thing, for instance – after she had ordered a grog. And when he'd gone, I asked her: By the way, isn't grog made with rum? In any other circumstances the prospect of imbibing a forty per cent alcohol drink, even diluted, would have made me prefer the firing squad, seeing that the devastating effects of the previous evening had not even begun to disperse, but I had a tendency to see things differently at present.

And yet, as the beauty sat a bit further back in her seat, there was nothing encouraging about what I saw in the mirror above the cracked, imitation-leather banquette: wet hair, plastered down by the cap which had left the imprint of a Merovingian crown over her ears, the wisp of hair slicked down over her forehead, and two curly ringlets framing a face with a nose red with cold, didn't have much in common with the more inviting idea of her that I had formed only a moment earlier. So everything was coming back to normal. Eviction from the domain of reverie. Return to the real. I lowered my head, as if I was afraid of inflicting such a vision on the beauty. And then, for the second time, a miracle. Theo, with both hands, which the moment before had been supporting her chin in the hollow of their palms, ruffled my hair, and, forcing me to look up at her, said: Well then, Jean-Arthur – what's going to happen to him?

I HAD MY OWN ROUGH idea, of course, but from that moment on I more or less lost interest in it. Writing takes place in solitude. Jean-Arthur had helped me get through a bad patch, but now that I had had a glimpse of something better I wasn't going to let him come between me and my budding amours. What did they both think? – that I was going to introduce them to each other and then discreetly step aside? None of that, Lisette, my father used to say, probably quoting a famous line of dialogue . . . famous at least in the Random theatre repertory. Jean-Arthur depended entirely on me, and on my good will, to save him from being tossed instanter into the waste-paper basket, where Gyf would certainly trample him underfoot with a nimble dance step after I and my violin had embarked on a Celto-Auvergnat air of my composition. As for the popular idea that fictional characters can escape from their author and do exactly what they like – just let him try. So I immediately settled his fate. If you really want to know, well, he dies. And now tell me about yourself.

Theo, finding that she had nothing much to say on the subject, soon returned to the attack. But why should he die? Like everyone else. There doesn't seem to be any particular reason why *he* should escape the common fate. And I wasn't talking without thinking. There was no underlying romanticism, nothing of the order of the abandoned, misunderstood artist who, rejected by the world, chooses to depart from it. No, no. He died just like people do, like my father did, like my Aunt Marie, like my grandfather, the tragic trinity of my twelfth year. And here, by an unprecedented phenomenon, the tears that I usually felt welling up just at the very mention of my blessed ones almost instantaneously flooded into the eyes of my charmer, as if she had taken it upon herself to remove the visible part of this grief that was too hard to bear. The teardrops soon trickled through the fine-tooth comb of her eyelashes and rolled down on to her cheekbones, had a magnifying effect on the little beauty spot, and died under the tips of her fingers at the corners of her mouth. Oh Theo, how sensitive you are, how sweet of you to be alarmed about me, how grieved you must be by the spectacle of the world, by all the misery everywhere, by people suffering and the revolution never coming, but don't cry, it's nothing, just see how I've got over it, how everything's all right now, my eyes are practically dry, and they would be completely dry if I wasn't sympathising with your sadness at my sadness, it's past history now, why should one waste time feeling sorry for oneself, harping on the same old wounds, when life can be so beautiful, so full of hope. But when she looked up at me, and her lovely, sad face so moved me that I had to stop myself clasping it in my hands, she gave me to understand that of course my story was something to cry about, but that wasn't exactly the reason for her tears. And I, put in my place for the hundred thousandth time, the place I should never try to venture out of, thought: Why is there never *anyone*, never any powerful outsider who feels enough compassion for me, for my weaknesses, for my lack of resources, to send me a telepathic message to tell me to think two hundred and twenty-two times before I open my mouth, instead of getting myself into disagreeable situations from which I systematically emerge at a disadvantage, with shame on my brow and discouragement in my heart. Why can I never learn except at my own expense, and it's true that that business of compassion didn't make sense, so it became apparent from her forlorn explanation that I had no exclusivity in this kind of tragedy and that fathers, they also died elsewhere, meaning hers, barely a year ago, and I was lucky if my wound had healed, hers was still open, and it hurt so much that she sometimes wanted to die.

Oh no, Theo, don't die, not now, we've only just got to know each other. But why did I need to liquidate my poor Jean-Arthur out of pure jealousy, the way you eliminate a rival, when he had had the immense merit of catching her attention. I should have cherished him, and returned the favour he had done me by granting him ten thousand years of life and even more. It was too late now to resuscitate him, the damage had been done, but even if I had, it wouldn't have brought Theo's father back. So I was expecting her to stand up and abandon me then and there with my steaming grog, whose very fumes turned my stomach, and when to my great surprise she remained seated, sadly pulling on a Virginia cigarette she had taken out of her bag, at the same time looking through the glass panel of the café door at the passers-by scuttling through the shower, I naturally resumed my favourite role, the one that worked best and for which I felt the most suited: the role of confidant, of Sister Œnone and Friar Leon.

Tell me then, Theo, you couldn't have picked anyone better. Fatherless people, when they meet, they're like the nobility, what have they got to say to one another?

Do you know, I've noticed that all my friends have a bit of a dodgy genealogy. It isn't an accident. People who haven't experienced it can't understand what it's like. What can you explain to them? Let them carry on living in clover. But we – we go hobbling along higgledy-piggledy, our hope crippled. All I have to do is round up the faithful shades from my memory to reconstruct this terror with you, and I'm with you. I know death like the back of my hand. I'll start, if that will help: With me, it was the day after Christmas.

With her it was one pancake day, at Candlemas. She had been singing while she whisked the batter, and dancing while she decorated the table with paper chains and candles, because her sick father was going to come home, cured. Her mother had gone to fetch him from his hospital a very long way away in the mountains. They had decided to allow him home to his family, which was a good sign, a sign that everything was going to return to normal. And so the batter was resting in its salad bowl when the car stopped at the front door. But when Theo rushed out, overjoyed, happy to be going to take the homecomer in her arms, her mother yelled at her not to come near. But that was quite in character, she was always shouting, whereas her father never raised his voice, or if he did it was very gently, and anyway he was asleep on the front seat, his head thrown back. That was just like him; he looked like an old child who was fast asleep. But actually, you understand, he wasn't asleep.

And Theo's tears began to flow even faster. For the last twenty kilometres, in what people often call "the dead man's place" – the front pasenger seat – her mother had been driving with a real dead man. And when Theo opened the door, rather as she had imagined doing, there was one essential difference, and the happy ending of her scenario turned into a nightmare – her father fell into her arms.

And now she wants to go. She suggests we go somewhere, anywhere, and why not to her place. She says she feels like carrying on – by which we should understand (or rather *I*, primarily, should understand), carrying on drinking, grog or whatever – with a look inviting my approval, which I interpret – this call to communion in only one kind – as a command. Whatever you say, Theo: straight ahead to hell.

Outside the café, when she has pulled the hood over her head again, she astonishes me by tenderly linking arms with me, which is the sort of gesture you normally associate with old couples and therefore belongs to the accoutrements of the perfect reactionary, but since it comes from her it's more like a lesson in strength and independence, a demonstration of her rarity. But my imprisoned arm, which after all I rather need in order to put my cap on, because the shower doesn't look as if it is going to let up – well, obviously, I wouldn't liberate it for anything in the world. And all the less so, seeing that I am soon going to owe to that slight inconvenience, the rain, the nicest possible gesture when, as soon as we get to her place and she sees me looking like a sopping wet cocker spaniel, she gets a towel and dries my hair with it. Before that, though, we go into a little grocer's shop where she sings out Hi! in such a charming manner to the grocer sighing in secret behind his counter, who probably spends the whole day waiting to see her, being obviously besotted with her; if not, why would he suggest that she pay for the little bottle of rum some other time, assure her that there's no hurry, refuse point blank the note I offer him, thus making sure of seeing her again, of sharing something with her, even if only a debt.

Reaching a vast freestone building, she tells me that her landlady is an old invalid, and that in exchange for an attic room, whose window we can see, she reads to her and does the odd chore: a bit of shopping, and answering her letters. This is why she asks me to walk on tiptoe in the corridor and when we go upstairs. The landlady's ears are not in such fine fettle as they once were, but she had come to an understanding with her young reader that visitors must be content to stay in the entrance hall. I was secretly delighting in this preferential treatment, already seeing it as a sign of special favour, when, at her express request to avoid a particular step that creaked, I realised that this exercise had already been repeated many times. Which cast a grey cloud over my rose-coloured sky.

Her room was lit by a dormer window which, in spite of the growing dusk, let in the golden light from a nearby street lamp. So you didn't need to switch the lights on in the room. She enjoyed, she explained, being in the semi-darkness, and even went so far as to move her chair up to the window when she felt like reading. The furniture, none of which matched, consisted of all the throw-outs from elsewhere in the house, but at least there was no shortage of armchairs, all of them period or reproduction. Yet it was her bed she got me to sit on while she was drying my hair. The water for the grog was heating in a saucepan on the stove (an ancient electric contraption with its element curling up in a spiral), the hum of the traffic on the boulevard below filled the silence, and I was trying hard to think of something intelligent to say, which didn't present itself, the definitive word that would console her for all her woes and assuage her grief.

For a fraction of a moment I thought about how she would reap what he, her father, had sown, but this time the All-powerful one advised me just in time to keep my prophecies to myself. And anyway, she had other things to tell me, and the best way for me to listen, no doubt, was for us to get more comfortable, because she had rapidly done my hair again, as she had in the café – something she seemed to be in the habit of – she tipped me backwards, almost making me knock my head against the wall, which involved a pull-up, followed by a rotation of ninety degrees, in order to make more judicious use of the length of the bed.

A narrow single bed, which meant that her head had to take refuge in the hollow of my shoulder if she didn't want to fall off, and this entitled me to become a bit bolder, and envisage twisting my neck round and possibly trying to kiss her, but, apart from the fact that it was in my interest to get her to forget my cavalier attitude of the previous evening, her eyes, perpetually on the verge of tears, made the situation seem so solemn that I understood how necessary it had been for us to lie down in order to take stock, to try to find a remedy for her torment. Besides, she kept saying that she had to tell me something, something she had never told anyone. A secret? I hazarded. But she was already on her feet, emptying the entire contents of the little bottle of rum into the saucepan, adding sugar, stirring it all together, and then, in a very egalitarian fashion, pouring it into two extra-large bowls like the ones that in the old days our butter used to come in, a very salty farm butter, decorated with a series of half-moons drawn with a wooden spoon.

For greater convenience, and so as not to scald ourselves, we soon found ourselves sitting up and gingerly sipping the steaming grog, and, considering our previous position, it seemed disastrously obvious to me that I had just missed a historic opportunity, as if one of the curves on the graph of our encounter had just passed through a tangential point and then curved back again, and moved away from the other for ever. Then, remembering the reason for my finding myself in this advantageous situation, without removing my lips from the bowl, timidly, courageously, I take the plunge and say: You wanted, I believe, to tell me something? But she doesn't answer, she takes refuge in a fumigation exercise over the strongly alcoholised vapours, and, as I am afraid she will regret having brought me to her room, that she will imagine that I am imagining things, that she will try and find a way of putting an end to the misunderstanding, I prefer to take the initiative. If the grog hadn't been so hot I would have knocked it back in one gulp, and, putting the bowl, which contained at least a litre, down on the little table by her bed, I would have thanked her warmly for the snack, really, with this weather, it was exactly what was needed, but goodness, time's getting on, looking at her alarm clock, that's to say peering at its face from twenty centimetres away, all that work I still have to do, and I'd have stood up hastily, thank you again, we'll probably bump into each other soon in the corridors or lecture rooms, in my headlong flight I would have made the accursed step creak as I went downstairs, the result being that the old invalid lady would have asked me what I was doing there, oh, nothing, Madame, nothing at all, please don't imagine, and then immediately have thrown her reader out for breach of contract, as a consequence of which the said reader would legitimately decide to exclude me from her life.

But I am so little in your life, Theo, we are the asymptotes that never meet, and anyway I'm not going to bother you any longer, I know you aren't on your own, I had an idea that you have a boyfriend, and I want to ask you to apologise to him for yesterday evening's incidents, the polluted bedspread, and it really is a pity that the grog doesn't cool more quickly, if it had I would already be down in the street without further ado. Only, all I manage to do is scald my oesophagus, which compels me to make certain contortions, whereupon she looks at me and smiles, a little grimace of a smile that I translate as: Poor boy, naive boy, silly boy, but which, guessing my state of mind, she immediately modifies: No harm done, she says.

And anyway, she had decided that she didn't want to see him any more, the boyfriend she was supposed to love, for a thousand and one reasons, the latest one, yesterday evening, being that he had been so nasty to me. Really? I wasn't so specially surprised, but that made me congratulate myself on having sent his bedspread to the cleaner's. Although I wouldn't want to be the cause of their splitting up, let me tell you that his insults leave me cold, and the proof of that is that I don't remember a thing. But it would certainly all sort itself out, and I was already offering myself as an intercessor when Theo put her bowl down on the little table and focused her lovely, sad gaze on me, her eyes glistening with tears. *Now* what have I said, O All-powerful one, that I shouldn't have?

It came out bit by bit, in dribs and drabs, between sobs. The sort of childhood tragedy that sometimes happens, which you try to bury deep down inside you, to file away with all the things that are over and done with, trivial, unimportant things, but they keep resurfacing and wounding you, tormenting you, they falsify everything, they drive everything to despair and forget nothing. They constitute a supernatural drama whose immaterial mark on your mind and body certainly lasts longer than any physical injury. Because nothing seems to remain of it, no visible scars, nothing life-threatening, and yet *something* is there, something is getting in the way, and has been doing its utmost to wreck everything ever since. And you – you who are on the receiving end of these fragments of fractured memory which cut like glass – all you can do is go on listening, silent and motionless, helpless, not even being allowed to offer a consoling word or a compassionate gesture, everything is inappropriate, you are required to be no more than an office where misery is recorded, a clerk of tears, a listening machine who looks on at suffering and resigns himself to being denied any share in it. But it's a promise, Theo, I won't say a word to anyone. It's your inner, painful self. It's nobody else's business.

Night had definitely fallen now, the golden light flooding in from the street had criss-crossed the floor with the magnified reflection of the squares of the casement window. Theo's sobbing spasms were becoming less frequent after her confession, and she got up and drew the little floral curtain across the brass rail, thus leaving us in a sort of dusky half-light, just enough to keep children's nocturnal terrors at bay, then she came and lay down again, propped her elbow on the pillow, her head in her hand, and with her other hand pulled me by the arm, inviting me to move closer, until we were face to face, just a few centimetres apart.

Hence the importance of the dim light coming through the curtain: I could see Theo's eyes glistening, her lovely, despairing, almost imploring eyes; she seemed prepared to trust any stranger who might be able to alleviate her torment. It was tempting to play that part, to become that person, the good Doctor Pangloss who cures the scrofula of the heart, and her mouth was so close that it was exactly like playing at doctors, that's to say, even for an awkward, timid person, child's play to traverse the few centimetres that separated me from that mouth. But I had barely had time to savour it when she quickly pulled away, distancing herself again, she still had things to tell me, she wanted everything to be absolutely clear, she wanted me to know where I stood so there wouldn't be any grey areas.

It seemed to me that after the first revelation the hardest part was over, that from then on I could hear everything, which I did, with the same attention, the same interest, and it's true that as I listened to her I felt she did indeed need to take stock, she had been so terribly affected by her father's death that she had become very officially engaged to a man much older than herself, then broken with him and accumulated various adventures, including feminine ones, so she felt a bit lost, and I understood that in the midst of this galaxy of cosmic complexity she was trying to explain that she would find it difficult to make room for me. Which showed great honesty on her part, even if I personally considered that my planetary conjunction was beginning to appear in a more favourable light. But, knowing how extremely changeable the sky is, being afraid I might have to wait a hundred and seven years for the next passage of my beautiful comet, I wondered whether it was really as flattering as she was trying to make out, the fact that she considered me different from the others, since the truth was that I wanted nothing more than to resemble the others who had held her in their arms.

Therefore, exploiting my role of confidant, longing with all my heart to join the common lot of normality, I ventured to slip my hand under her black sweater which she wore next to her skin, and this same hand, delicately feeling its way up her back, soon came up against the hook of a bra. An event that threw some light on Theo's nature, because her behaviour, which people – not very close observers – could mistakenly have attributed to the ongoing sexual revolution (whose start she maintained I had missed out on), didn't at all square with the far less rigid ideas of dress of the said revolution. So Theo had a sense of decorum. Hence, reassured by this discovery, I was prepared to listen to the ultimate secret. For there was still one last thing (her mouth had once again retreated, and I was beginning to get a little tired of being constantly interrupted). Yes, Theo? No, this time she was too ashamed. Oh come on, tell me, what *couldn't* I hear, now? Together we had leafed through the most secret, the most intimate pages of the diary of her wounds, what coda, what explanatory note could throw a new light on her big sad eyes? It could only be some minor item, shameful maybe, but which came within the normal cycle of the ups and downs of life.

I felt my powers of empathy faltering, even showing some signs of impatience, now that the tips of my fingers had encountered the texture of her skin. Tell me everything then, Theo, and let's say no more about it, let's stop this cruel ballet between your mouth and mine. She hesitated, and then, after a moment's thought, said no, really not, and I wasn't to insist. I tried to get her back on track as I had done before. Was it serious? Would she get over it? Would it have consequences? No, no, whatever was I imagining, and anyway she was sorry she had committed herself unnecessarily, and in any case it was no big deal, and then it was her business, after all. I hadn't asked any questions, but whatever you like, Theo. And at the same time as we were moving towards a new rapprochement I was imagining the worst, going through a catalogue of the unavowable: sleeping with a professor to find out about exam questions? going on the game? marrying a banker? compromising herself with a judge? joining the police? But that could come later, because Theo had her arms in the air and was taking off her sweater and, what with the white cups of her bra suddenly piercing the semi-darkness, you can well imagine that there were other things to think about.

THE NEXT DAY, YOU are annoyed with yourself. Not because of what happened, for which you give thanks to Theo, to heaven and to the whole world, but because you behaved like an idiot. Not with the beauty, obviously – there we (the modest royal we) sinned more through an excess of delicacy – but with time: at not having been capable of savouring every instant, fully, successively, at its true value. Take the white cups, for example, like two book ends for carnal knowledge, which hollow out that furrow-funnel in which gaze, light, and desire are engulfed as in a black hole, with their narrow straps perpendicularly crossing the clavicles. On reflection, everything happened too quickly. Why such haste with the hook on her back, why such obstinacy, however delicate, in undoing it, why such triumph, however humble, in pulling it off so rapidly instead of enjoying in slow motion this efflorescence, this liberation of the two caged breasts which, once the hook has been bisected, abandon themselves to gravity, with a brown semi-halo sticking out above the lace of the cup, like the midnight sun emerging from the whiteness, the straps slowly gliding over her arms while her shoulders seem to want to shrink, they retract as if to slide through a narrow passage, and extract themselves by a seasoned illusionist's contortion from the cangue of the satin-smooth fabric, in the process causing a compression of the central furrow between the breasts, the arms liberating themselves one after the other – and, even before I had hollowed my hands to cradle those twin pearls of water, which made her attention wander for a moment to look at the bra on the floor, there it lay, abandoned like a cocoon shed by the wings of a butterfly, and yet so rich in kept promises. And that's only one example. You can imagine the rest.

And so you are annoyed with yourself. You would like to rewind it, to show the evening's film again in slow motion, pausing on the image, becoming a dual personality, leaving your body, and you would like to do this, another example, so as to enjoy the sight of the recumbent beauty's legs wrapped round your waist, a sight which necessarily escaped you since it happened behind your back, and anyway, at the same time you were gazing into her wide-open eyes. But it was obviously something very wonderful. And also a thousand other delightful things. Which ought to be seen again, then. And the best way, unless you can find the key to putting the clock back, is to do it again.

Which is why the next day (even though the night before had been short: the reader, afraid of being caught, had turned you out as two o'clock was striking, which meant that since you weren't allowed to put the stair light on you did in fact make the famous step creak, the fifth one, yet not for lack of warning, and in theory counting up to five isn't so very difficult, but you probably left on the wrong foot) you come back. You can't remember what you agreed on when you parted: Shall we see each other again, yes, no, maybe, tomorrow, some other day, or did she want time to think about it? For yourself, no need to rack your brains, no question about it: you do want an encore. And yet you begin to feel a little doubtful as you approach the big stone building, shivering in your navy blue reefer jacket which hasn't had time to dry in these few hours, because the nocturnal return was accomplished on foot, in the rain, there being no buses at that hour, and as for taking a taxi – think again. And what if your welcome didn't come up to your expectations? What if your two minds, which for a moment had espoused one another, had branched off instead of advancing jointly? No, though, you weren't dreaming, after all.

You weren't dreaming. To reassure yourself of that you put a hand on your shoulder which is still aching from the beauty's savage bite, but you are soon going to find out that sleeping on it didn't give us both the same advice. You haven't got long now before your illusions vanish. Just the time it takes for Theo to come downstairs and open the door after you've pressed the little copper button ensconced in its marble orbit, and for her to discover you, look amazed, and mime a pout: Ah, it's you. Of course, who else? Well, for example, it could be the fellow you didn't see arriving on your heels and at whom, over your shoulder, she is aiming a broad smile, as if you had suddenly become transparent. So you turn round and instantly hate him. Even if he had made a good impression when your eyes met you would have hated him just as much for that smile intended for him, but he has the extraordinary nerve to consider that it is you who are the perfect intruder, and from a height (he takes shameful advantage of being a head taller than you), because after all who came first, and of the two of us, who is the importuner, the impostor, the incredible malapert, the non-respecter of precedence? But just because he has the face of an angel, curly hair and blue eyes, he needn't expect *me* to see him as one of the Good Lord's holy innocents. Although the Good Lord would do well to take him in hand; a few sharp moral lessons from the Master could do him nothing but good – but Theo? And Theo, why does she go on smiling at him every time their eyes meet, whereas she keeps her weeping-woman look for me, the air of the eternal torture victim whose wounds I had undertaken to heal, one by one? Who is this charlatan, this medicine-man who returns her smile while I am stuck there playing gooseberry? She introduces Diego. A Spanish friend, she feels obliged to add.

Obviously, with a name like that, but I didn't remember her mentioning him in her second confession as being one of her suitors – of whichever sex. Among those vernacular Christian names, an exotic touch wouldn't have escaped me. But it wasn't physically possible for her to have had time to pull this one ex nihilo out of her hat during the morning, and it wasn't I who had made him miraculously appear like an evil genie by ringing a bell. So she must have deliberately tried to hide him from me. The third confession? But was there really anything to be ashamed of in having a lover from the other side of the Pyrenees? Or else, and I could see no other solution, he was one of Franco's grandsons. That explained everything. Nothing to boast about, indeed. To confess such a malfeasance to a fellow traveller along the route of the Mongo-Aoustinian cause would be to condemn yourself to an appearance before a People's Tribunal – and the people show no leniency to their class enemies. She was certainly risking a lot: expulsion from her cell, or something of the sort.

And yet there was one point that bothered me. Ashamed, maybe, but she seemed to be fond of her Falangist, excusing herself to him with a tender look while she takes me by the arm and leads me aside on the pavement, explaining to me that she wants to explain to me. What, Theo? I'm not a complete fool, I can use my eyes, I may not have very good sight but even so I'm not blind. You're free to compromise yourself with the garrotters, the proletarian revolution will know how to recognise its friends, but when the time comes that Mongo-Aoustinian thought enlightens the world I shall do everything in my power to prevent them shaving off your beautiful hair, my dearest Theo. Or perhaps I shall gather it up and bury my face in it, and through its perfume relive the blessed hours of our night together, weeping for my beautiful lost love. But don't bother to get out your kid gloves to tell me what is patently obvious, go back quick to your hidalgo and don't worry about me, I have some wonderful memories, and they'll last me a long time. With far less than that, with just a few fuzzy images of a pretty girl who drowned, I furnished my reveries over long years. So you can imagine that with what you gave me I have enough to last me for an eternity.

Will you let me know how Jean-Arthur is getting on? Without fail, Theo, but I'm afraid that from now on things aren't going to turn out so well for him, and that his matrimonial projects with his friend's sister are going to fall through. But you must leave me now, I'm going to have to cry.

That obsession with tears – it was a good opportunity: an unhappy love affair, or at least no one could deny that it rather looked like one – they had no hesitation in flowing, sure of their legitimacy, hardly under suspicion of senti-mentality, this time they were in a noble cause. They overdid it a bit, perhaps, as if they were taking advantage of the situation, like firemen always on the alert in the hope of provoking a huge fire for them to put out and never mind who started it, as if their zeal was merely the expression of a physiological need for effusion, as if they were making the most of this heaven-sent opportunity although basically they didn't care a damn about my chagrin. The result was that this suspicion of insincerity, this reflex of the great tragediennes, made me doubt the true nature of my feelings. For even if, at the stage I'd got to, as I was slowly walking away from the big stone building, my back bowed under the weight of my affliction, I felt that I had the soul of an old adventurer, heart broken and skin tanned, I shouldn't lose sight of the fact that this encounter, after all, simply amounted to two evenings (the first of which I had not the slightest recollection of), which had encompassed a day during which I was above all engaged in fighting off the devastating effects of the Gyfian mixtures. Was that enough to justify inventing a whole epic?

A mystery did remain, though: what can I have talked about in my alcoholic delirium to make the beauty, despite my cavalier attitude, choose me for her confidant? What words uttered by me between attempts at stolen kisses, had persuaded her to let me into the secret of what lay behind the façade of her sad eyes? For nothing had forced her to worry about my health the next day and accompany Gyf to my cell, nor, once there, to take the most humble measures to clean the place up and remove all traces of the previous evening's transgressions. As unlikely as it may seem, she had wanted, she, Theo of the white cups and black eyes, to see me again, me, Jean-Arthur, with my Cyclopean spectacles. Which means that in her thoughts, I had for a few hours played the unhoped-for part of the person she had hoped for. However, from there to extolling the virtues of an alcoholic disturbance of the senses would be to leave out of account the cataclysmic aftermath, which would certainly serve as a deterrent until the next time. But in the end, as my natural state had naturally disappointed her, it was disappointing to disappoint, and not to be the one, the hidalgo, for example, who wins the day. So I didn't necessarily stand to gain by hanging around in the neighbourhood with slumped shoulder, making a pitiful show of my alleged broken heart. Better to make a quick getaway, all the more so as they seemed to be in such a hurry to be together again that I didn't imagine they would be watching me until I disappeared round the corner; I was practically certain that Franco-Spanish friendship had already made great strides, effortlessly avoiding the fatal step.

Even more than my tears, though, what indicated my disillusion was my haste to get away from the scene and the way I kept accelerating my pace until I was soon running, faster and faster and faster, yet not to the point of having to gasp for breath: on the contrary, I had the impression that my breath was inexhaustible and that my feet were barely touching the pavement, just as it is in my dreams, where it is so easy for me to walk in a state of weightlessness, levitating a few metres and getting a purchase on the air with my folded arms outstretched, my thumbs under my groin, thus effortlessly advancing above the ground. Breathlessness and fatigue had so little effect on me that I couldn't understand why those carefully-timed races at school had left me with memories of such agony. The streets flashed by, like those sequences in a film seen through the rear window of a stationary car; I followed them blindly, slaloming between vehicles as I dodged across the congested roads, never keeping to the pedestrian crossings, jumping over unexpected obstacles –

such as crates outside a grocer's shop – in my haste barging into any passers-by who were too dopy to get out of the way of this semi-maniac who didn't even tell them to watch out, who didn't even hear the car drivers' admonishments, their horns, their curses; who couldn't even see.

For my horizon had shrunk even further. The tears obstructing the remaining tenths of my vision made my marathon even more aleatory, and diluted the last impressions of the real – a few red dots – with which I normally constituted my chart of the sky for terrestrial use. And since the speed I was running at made it impossible for me to get anything into focus, the world revealed itself only when it threw itself upon me, so I felt I was moving inside a thousand-faceted crystal. Theo's face interposed itself between my mind and this world of hazy appearances, and in its turn lost its resolution, so I had to mobilise all my thoughts to bring it back, and when it seemed it had gone for ever I applied myself to recomposing it, starting from one precise element, the little beauty spot for instance, and from there I had a go at her smile, the way she screwed up her eyes, the intense brilliance of her gaze, but her features soon vanished again until I finally began to doubt what really had happened, like young Bernadette, in her Nevers convent, no longer very sure that she had genuinely seen the tall white lady in her grotto in the hamlet of Massabielle, or Joan of Arc, during her trial, incapable of swearing that she had indeed heard the three heavenly voices above that supernatural tree, Joan, who, back in her cold tower in Rouen, must have wondered whether honestly it was worth while risking the stake for some dubious voices. Maybe I had simply been content to borrow some of Theo's features to nourish my reverie, as I had done with my drowned girl. There was one difference, though: I had evidence, very real evidence this time: the deep impression left in my flesh by the teeth of the beauty, who, like a fairy godmother, really had bent over my shoulder. I had at least that certainty. Which obviously didn't give any indication of what was to follow. And perhaps after all it was only her personal vampirish way of leaving her mark on her suitors. Without going any further. Anaesthetised by the grogs, still suffering the consequences of the previous evening's excesses which had caused me that ablation of several hours of my existence, their hallucinatory effects might well have persisted. Perhaps I was only just beginning to emerge from a long foggy crossing by finding my footing again on the few hectometres of asphalt that my extraordinary gait needed.

This was how, still running, I soon bumped into a crowd, which I pushed through in spite of the protests of its members, shoving my way between the densely-packed bodies and then, ducking under a cordon of linked hands, emerging on to an open space, a vast cobbled square without a sign of traffic and strangely deserted at that hour, darting alone across this unbounded, unobstructed ground, and it seemed as if I was being welcomed into an arena that was on the scale of the immensity of my suffering over my lost love. And that is when, as so often happens, I became aware of the little grain of sand against which reveries and the best constructs of the imagination tend to stumble: I was only just beginning to be surprised by this anomaly, this absence of traffic jams and pedestrians in a place usually so full of both, that, jerked out of the battleground of my thoughts, I tripped over an unexpected object and fell flat on my face on the cobblestones, just managing to catch the few words someone was yelling, something like look at that moron, or imbecile, or triple idiot, but in any case nothing very complimentary, whereas it would have been more legitimate for them to be concerned for my wellbeing. Hadn't I hurt myself? broken anything? for it had certainly been an impressive crash-landing on the cobbles.

And in fact, the pain in my knee was so acute that it took me back to my Jean-Arthur. This was probably out of a sort of resentment, but I was also thinking that I would allow him to benefit from my pain. Because after all, what did he expect, that cripple? That when he came back from his wanderings he would be welcomed with open arms? That every woman would throw herself on his neck? That everyone would listen spellbound to his tales of a son of the desert? Didn't he know that such home-comings are improbable and bode no good? Now that I was going to have time, now that nothing and nobody would be permitted to distract me from my great work, I promised myself that I would take him up again. And, as my pain spread, I decided there and then that I was going to plunge the savage invalid into a cryogenic coma from which there was very little chance that the beauty, even by a bite on the shoulder, would ever come and deliver him.

But the man was insisting, the unsympathetic fellow whose black boots with cleated soles I could see approaching. And as I looked up at him I saw that he was burning with enthusiasm, buttoned up tight in a heavy leather jacket and wearing a helmet that looked like a monstrance, from which – from this accoutrement – I identified him as a specialist in the fight against fires, but it didn't even occur to me to find his presence disturbing, and I turned my head to look for the cockeyed cobblestone that had caused my downfall, but in the matter of cobblestones there was nothing to be seen but a whacking great hosepipe blocking the square. My next reflex was to look to my right to see where the said pipe went, and I observed that a few metres farther on it left the ground and snaked up to a ladder on top of a red fire engine, and at the top of this ladder were two firemen clinging on to the hose for dear life, trying to resist the violent pressure of the water spurting out of it, a powerful jet that culminated in an arc and came splashing down over the roof of Saint Peter's Cathedral.

But where the roof had been, there was already nothing left but its framework, outlined by shafts of fire, from which gigantic flames leapt up, twisting into spindles, lacerating the dusk, sometimes giving the impression of bending under the pressure of the water, then springing up even more fiercely and mounting an onslaught on the winter sky. The calcinated beams crashed down into the inferno, whose roar drowned out the orders being yelled by a man in uniform. The stained-glass windows of the nave were now no more than reddening, gaping wounds, as if on this Whitsun in reverse, weary of preaching love in the wilderness, the wounded Spirit was leaving this world.

So I had a ringside seat, I was a witness blinded by a thousand little sparks in his eyes whom the unsympathetic fellow now ordered to shove off, and the strangest thing of all was that instead of being amazed at the disaster, or deploring the fact that such a prestigious edifice should go up in smoke – although basically this was certainly the right day – as I started running again, half-limping, after one last look at the flames, I thought: Theo, why have you forsaken me?

IV

GYF MUST FINALLY HAVE disposed of his collection of family silver, or perhaps have looted the sacristy in Logrée, because he received an unexpected windfall and used it to take his film – or his serial proposition, or iconographic apparition, or oneiric fulmination – to be developed. All he had to do now was work on the sound track – or auditory space, or acoustic compulsion, or vibratory problematics – because the musicians around the bed of love had in fact been content to mime, having not the slightest knowledge of the instruments they were supposed to be playing, and in any case at that time the film maker – or unifier of images, or clarifier of volumes, or duplicator of light – didn't possess a tape recorder, so that the violin, for instance (which was a pasteboard imitation), might just as well have been entrusted to La Fouine, although the Weasel's uncontrollable side might perhaps have upset the lovemaking of the actors – or physiological vectors, or mediumistic references, or long-distance screwers – in their great love scene (or sexual imbrication, or cellular fusion, or spatio-temporal cantata). My role – to which I owed Gyf's visit – consisted in setting this mute score to music, and that was why, now that the film or whatever you like to call it was at last visible, I had brought my violin, so that as soon as the match was over I could see the preview of *Tomb for Grandmother*.

With the black violin case strapped perpendicularly on

to the luggage rack of the Solex, my sports bag wedged between my legs, my feet propped up on the little footrest, the map of the route to the grandmaternal farm taped on to the handlebars, I found it even more awkward to steer a straight course because the road was wet and, in such conditions, apart from the risk of skidding, the cylinder driving the front wheel had a tendency to slip, so that, all the time pedalling more vigorously, I had to press down on the engine with the black Bakelite knob of the lever sticking up out of the cylinder, in order to keep the motor unit in contact with the wet tyre. Otherwise the engine began to race in neutral, bringing you to a standstill rendered perilous by the uncertain equilibrium of the whole shebang, on account of the centre of gravity being too high.

None of which prevented me from singing at the top of my voice and soliloquising out loud, as I did every time, regaling the aerial elements with my most profound thoughts, my most intimate torments, even allowing myself to hurl abuse at the odd pedestrian or cyclist who foolishly got in my way, sure of my impunity, since the speed I was going at plus the noise of the engine would drown out – or so I convinced myself – my vehement remarks. But they didn't in fact drown them out, for I soon realised that it had been a mistake to qualify as a stupid peasant a farmer who came out of his yard pushing a wheelbarrow full of manure, into which I should probably have landed had I not made the bold adjustment of the handlebars which took me into his farmyard, obliged me to circumvent a well, slalom between his hens and re-emerge, pedalling harder than ever, past the menacing fist of the master of the establishment.

Once out of reach of the irascible farmer I resumed my

solitary reflections, improvising words to the appropriate tune, such as: The sun has got his hat on, / Hip hip hip hooray, / Theo bit my shoulder / But she chucked me the next day. Or again: Everything's going my way. Or even: Pack up your troubles in your old kitbag. Because if I considered, for instance, my companionship with La Fouine, whom I had just left at the village square and who had sworn, ever since I had trusted him with my violin, that our friendship would last until death us did part, I saw two possibilities opening out before me: either to recognise the familiar but now insistent secret little smile from destiny in it, or to sink into the lowest depths of despair. But the fog that had permanently engulfed me since my serial bereavements and since I had stopped wearing glasses, still didn't allow me to see my way with any certainty. And so, calling on the heavens to bear witness to my misfortune, I apostrophised a pallid moon floating around through the owl-light. Get a move on with your lantern, O etiolated Moon, light my path, or I'll send a great big black sun up into your sky to make your sad Pierrot face even whiter, and the stars in comparison will look like dwarf fireflies, ephemeral sparks from the flint of a cigarette lighter, because *my* star illumines my Empyrean with blazing thunderstorms, inflames the mass of shadows, makes winter nights iridescent, melts the ice fields of our hearts. And as the world is like an ice cream sandwiched between the poles, it won't be a great devastating conflagration, but the white devil, the specialist of subdolous death, that will carry us away into its desert-in-reverse, and that is why, O pale peaky Moon, aborted boiler, lorgnette, cold stone, I am going to tell you the name of your great rival, she who will put you back in your place – that of a sterile egg yoke – and will turn the Milky Way into a river of milt to inseminate the Universe with its Théological beauty. Make room, you creatures of the night, clear a way in space, prepare to welcome a great prodigy: a new star is born, brighter than Vega, more beautiful than Cassiopeia, more luminous than Altair: Gloria in excelsis Theo. And I only withdrew from my interior planetarium in order to put a foot on the ground in front of the signposts and stick my nose up against the blue enamel of the little arrows pointing with their white letters to the hamlets.

This was how, having familiarised myself with the toponomy (The Black Hedges, The Devil's Hump, and similar Invitations to the Voyage), having gone round in circles for a good hour and systematically explored the byroads of the Logréean countryside – and some of them several times – , finally, by pure chance, I came across the farm of the grandmother with the erotic tomb, and it became more and more apparent to me that this grandmother had a good deal to answer for. The description her pious heir had given me left no room for doubt: the letterbox nailed up on a post at the entrance to the path bore the words Paradox and Equivocality, which were supposed to inform the postman of the patronymics of Gyf and his latest girlfriend, without precisely stating which was Paradox and which Equivocality, although both were certainly members of the Ambiguous family.

It was a little single-storey house with an adjoining cowshed, like thousands of others in the countryside north of the Loire, extending lengthwise, with a slate roof and two windows on either side of a stable door – its lower half could be shut independently and thus keep animals from inviting themselves into the kitchen. Gyf, when he spoke about it, was somewhat inclined to exaggerate its bucolic character, its telluric powers, its restorative qualities; words failed him, he said. But even before I went into the house I could already have described its low ceiling, the smoke-blackened exposed beams, the mud floor, the coke stove, and the table covered with a sticky oilcloth that hung down on to the knees of the guests sitting on benches on either side. This didn't demand any profound knowledge of the local customs and habitat on my part: we used to get our milk from a farm just like it in the old days, thanks to which, after watching the cows being milked (this growing lad, taking advantage of being left on his own, used to send a powerful jet of milk flying across the cowshed, thus establishing a new long-distance record), I had discovered some practices we had never heard of (such as turning your plate upside down to show you wanted to continue the meal), on our way home we couldn't wait to verify the effects of centrifugal force (and thus understand the move-ment of the planets) by whirling the milk churn round in circles at arm's length without spilling a drop – apart from the one occasion when we had to go back and get it filled up again.

Gyf's grandmother had made a few improvements, in particular by having the mud floor covered with cement, but basically the interior decoration was of the period (in particular the lintel along the mantelpiece, trimmed with red-and-white-check gingham, and the highly character-istic lampshade in white frosted glass, a flattened cone with a transparent fluted border, equipped with a pear-shaped, ceramic counterweight filled with little lead pellets so you could adjust its height), the touch of the present owner being recognisable by the utter chaos that reigned and could have been the death of anyone – for instance, a hen who had taken it into her head to try to find her chicks therein.

Gyf was well aware of this, and he asked me to ignore it. But that was difficult, unless you closed your eyes and perhaps even held your nose: several days' dishes were stagnating in the sink, the antique stove bore the stigmata of several centuries of cooking, and the breakfast coffee bowls were still on the table together with the cat's dish, the latter sitting on someone's lecture notes. The walls were hung with tea towels painted in the expressionist manner (when I ventured to ask the painter about the symbolism of that thistle crowned with a UFO, I could have kicked myself for not having immediately recognised Che and his famous beret), in a corner there was a broom dressed up as a puppet, and in a leather armchair whose springs had obviously had it, given the low level of its occupants, the cat was asleep on the knees of either Paradox or Equivocality, but she was a pretty blonde whose long, fine hair framed a transparent face. Which once again raised the lancinating question: how on earth did Gyf, decked out in such glasses, manage to seduce such beauties?

He had also invited a guitarist friend with whom I was supposed to create not so much a score – what an idea – as an ambience, who drew attention to himself on arrival by a noise like thunder (the crunch of corrugated iron). And anyway, his first words when he came in were to ask who owned the Solex that was so badly parked in the yard and which he had only seen too late, but the owner needn't worry, there didn't seem to be any damage. Introducing myself as the said owner, who all the same *was* worried (now that I could establish a link between the din and my moped), I rushed outside. His Citroën 4L, parked in front of the barn, more or less skilfully decorated, according to whether you thought in terms of action painting or envisaged a long halt under a scaffolding on which house painters were plying their trade), lacked a right wing, and was certainly much more to be pitied than my Solex, even though, once I had propped it back up on its stand, I did nevertheless have to straighten the handlebars, clamping the front wheel between my thighs, which didn't do my trousers any good, the result being that when I went back into the kitchen my feelings towards the newcomer were somewhat mixed.

All the more so as, turning the musical situation to his own advantage, he hadn't waited for me. Crouching over his guitar, he had started on a long threnody of his own composition which said: Mama, Mama, can I have a banana, which went round and round in never-ending circles which, he explained, when after a moment we suggested he might change his tune a bit, was based on the method of Indian ragas, which he had of course adapted to his own way of playing and remixed with various influences, in particular Afro-pre-Columbian ones (you might as well say America before the discovery of the Bering Strait), and also folk-ethnological ones (he had recorded his grandfather in a Logréean version of *Les Filles de Camaret*). Personally, I recognised the king-kong system: Mama, Mama = king; can I have a banana = kong. But seeing that my musical culture wasn't on a par with that of my new friend, I was quite proud to discover that I, all alone in my little corner, *I* had built a bridge between the Orient and the Occident, and as he was considering adding a few words and casually asked me for a contribution (Gyf must have mentioned my Jean-Arthur), I suggested: Can I have – why not a chipolata, or a strawberry melba, or some gorgonzola (in so far as you weren't limited to a choice of *either* cheese *or* dessert). Mama didn't agree, so we moved into the next room to watch *Tomb for Grandmother.*

Gyf had rigged up the cowshed as an auditorium, which wasn't immediately apparent if you were expecting padded seats and a stage hung with crimson velvet. The room could quite easily have been returned to its original function. The feeding troughs were still lined up along the wall, and it was easy to see that the wooden partitions between the stalls had been used to botch up the platform that served as a stage, in front of which were about a dozen chairs, some of which were made of chromium-plated tubular metal interlaced with strips of red plastic and in all probability came from the waiting room of an outpatients' department. According to the master of ceremonies, they held poetic evenings there – poetic being understood in its widest sense. Which is? Poetry is everywhere except in poetry, Gyf retorted, in an unanswerable, very Paradox-Equivocality tone of voice, as he swept away any literary miasmata with the back of his hand. Since I was feeling a little sorry for my Jean-Arthur, I insisted on further information. Well, in the last show, for instance, there had been a recording made covertly inside the hold of a cargo boat under construction. But, to Gyf's regret, the dock workers hadn't shown up. Whereas for *La Belle et la Bête* he had had to turn people away. Did it follow the text of Madame Leprince de Beaumont? Not exactly: a girl had undressed while a sheep was being sheared beside her. I observed that it was a great pity I hadn't been there with my violin to accompany the performance. You remember, Gyf: the fleeces of our sheep, tra la, 'tis we as wields the shears, while I tried out a few dance steps borrowed from La Fouine. But as he seemed less than a hundred per cent enthusiastic, I pointed out the permanent presence of

204

erotico-bucolic themes in his oeuvre, whereupon he told me I hadn't seen anything yet – which was true – and asked Madame Ambiguous to bring him a sheet, the one from the bed would do, while he loaded the projector and then set it up on a stool in the middle of the room.

The sheet had been slept on, and when it was hung over the platform with the light focused on it you could even detect the origin of some of its stains, but Gyf stated categorically that it was the most beautiful backcloth he had ever seen, and it reminded him of that Chinese or Siamese or Korean painter from whichever dynasty it was who used to dip his brush in the tears of his mistress. From which delicate evocation it would become easier for us to understand that this *art brut* demonstrated that art was above all an act of love, and moreover that it was the act of love that had given him the idea of elaborating on the theme of Life's Miracles: a collective exhibition for which everyone would bring his own sheet – before it had been washed – which would show that creation, formerly confiscated by the property-owning class and its pseudo art markets, is in reality within the reach of everyone. And, after Paradox-Equivocality had switched off the lights, a luminous disc projected a tondo on to the holy shroud.

In the foreground was a schoolboy's slate with *Tomb for Grandmother* written on it, although as I couldn't see it clearly I couldn't really read it, but you could guess that much. Then Gyf in person rubbed out the text, chalked something in its place and turned the slate over so that all you could see was a black rectangle, closely followed by a blinding shot: the camera was filming the sun, the sky, a bird in flight, the tops of the trees, then it slowly descended and focused on an empty bed plumb in the middle of a field, a high, old-fashioned bed with dark wooden posts and, according to Gyf, it was in this very bed that he had been conceived. After which a piece of gauze was interposed in front of the camera, gently floating in the breeze, through which you could glimpse the silhouettes of a man and a woman. The couple were walking, holding hands, still protected by the tightly-stretched gauze, which you then discovered was being held at arms' length by the musicians and a few girls wearing long skirts and nothing on top. When they reached the bed the gauze dropped, and while the naked lovers were climbing up on to their couch the girls danced around and the musicians formed a circle and began to play. I had to reconstitute this, because the camera was quite a long way from the bed and I was too far away from the screen, not daring to move my chair up any closer in case anyone might think my interest in the scene was anything other than purely artistic, but at the moment when Gyf's film took on its full meaning, however hard I blinked, the mysterious beauty only revealed herself through her halo of mist.

I acknowledged, though, that Gyf had been right: the so-called Yvette, identifiable by her heavy head of hair, certainly was on top. Then the camera, which I was hoping would either zoom or track in, having at first remained at a chaste distance where it lingered on the lovers, once again ascended to the treetops, the sky, the sun, and there was another blackout. The slate had been turned back but this time, not knowing the text, I was incapable of deciphering the Gyfian prose. However, when the lights came on again and I turned round to look at the director, he gave me a little nod, as if seeking my approval – a sort of: Don't you agree? I hesitated for a moment, afraid of muffing it, then I nodded back in the same way: a sign that yes, I did agree.

Then equivocality and paradox left the auditorium, arm in arm, without a word of comment, just Gyf's request to the guitarist: Don't forget to switch off the projector when you've finished. Then they climbed up the miller's ladder leading to the loft which they had converted into their bedroom, probably wanting to waste no time in recording the score of their amorous sighs, while I was to synchronise my violin with the whimsical bowing of the improvised musician.

Gyf – your specs – you're myopic, aren't you? Gyf stops half way up the ladder, surprised to see me down at the bottom, reluctantly allowing his companion's long skirt to disappear through the rectangle cut into the ceiling between two rafters and, unenthusiastically looking down at me from on high, asks me why I ask – was the film out of focus? No no, well, actually yes, but only for me, I'm too shortsighted to see the screen clearly, I need a few more centimetres, but if you were myopic too, Gyf, I'd be very glad, for myself, of course, because it's a handicap and I wouldn't wish it on anyone else, except you maybe, because in that case if you would lend me your specs they'd be a great help, then I wouldn't bow out of synch, it's a question of the violin of course, nothing to do with girls, don't start imagining things, we're working in the interests of art . . . and Gyf, taking off his glasses, asks: Do you know her? Who are you talking about?

But he too disappears through the ceiling, snapped up by those impatient, outstretched arms which wrest him from the sight of the Groundlings, and this abduction crowns the solitude of the one who remains earthbound, heavier than air, diminished, head bowed, putting on those improbable glasses: the curved bit at the end of their side-pieces consists of a spiral spring that fits round the back of the ears and cuts into the flesh, which explains why their lenses lie flat against the eye sockets and produce a little crease above the cheekbones, so you feel as if you were wearing a welder's prosthesis since it is virtually impossible to rub your eye by introducing a finger between the glass and your eyelid. Apart from this aesthetic detail, however, it's true that you can see better. From this moment on you identify yourself with Kaspar Hauser emerging from his cave, you feel you are setting out to discover the world. You start with a rapid exploration of your property, the upshot of which is that the state of the kitchen was more acceptable when seen through blurred vision, which usually shows more indulgence to filth, wrinkles, and similar imperfections. Instead of which, once you have moved into the third dimension and see in relief a bit of bread on the table, which suddenly becomes enigmatic, or the circles of wine left on the wood by the stems of the wine glasses, nothing escapes you. The result is that you become critical, everything provides a reason for a more or less caustic comment: the walls could do with a coat of paint, the floor needs sweeping, and the ceiling would look a lot better without its cobwebs. Even Che, who frankly looks less like a thistle now, appears even more ridiculous with his UFO on his head.

But you haven't come to the end of your woes as a sighted person. There remains the ordeal by mirror.

The one hanging on a little chain looped round a nail near the door to the so-called projection room. Well, you haven't yet reached the stage when you can walk along a pavement without looking at your reflection in shop windows, when you can simply ignore your reversed double. Whenever a mirror appears there is a confrontation, a cruel face-to-face encounter, the mortifying, discouraging: Is that *me*? Really? Couldn't you come up with something else? And maybe without the glasses I would never even have noticed that little mirror framed in its spherical, chromium-plated beading with a crack at the bottom right-hand corner revealing a bit of grey cardboard, but there was a sudden moment of terror when you lowered your eyes and went out through the stable door: there was a Gyfian avatar in the mirror.

And clear vision is unforgiving. The idea of yourself that you have lived with in your misty introversion, which you have adapted to as best you can, which you end up considering almost acceptable – suddenly, there it is, impeached, laminated, annihilated: that specimen with the appalling glasses, the long hair plastered down with sweat, the unshaven cheeks, the one you pitied when it was Gyf, well, it's no good trying to kid yourself, that specimen is you. And you would immediately have put the ghastly glasses down on the table if the guitarist hadn't called you at that moment to tell you that he had set up the film again, and even asked you to put the lights out, which suits you fine, and anyway, if you had to go around with that sorrowful countenance for ever, you would do better to settle for a permanently subterranean life in the depths of a cave, just barely tolerating the flickering glimmer of an oil lamp to light the hand holding the charcoal and drawing a hymn to beauty on the wall.

But the guitarist is once more calling his Mama. I interrupt him and suggest he plays his two chords again – or his Logrée-Amerindian raga, if he prefers, but this time without the text – and I would undertake to improvise to them. And Gyf has already written his secret phrase on the slate, another blackout, then comes the sun with those little spermatozoids wriggling all over the film. Now you can see everything of the bird in its flight, and you don't need much ornithological knowledge to identify it – the gracious movement of its wings casually beating down on the air (nothing in common with my dreams of flight) – and then come the trees, and you notice at once that they are not simply a fibrous, chlorophyllous, anonymous mass. And the bed: obviously a grandmother's bed, heavy, massive, with ornate posts, like the one that Sean Thornton takes to his thatched, whitewashed cottage for his wedding night with Mary Kate Danaher, a bed, as Gyf had rightly emphasised, suited for conception, and no doubt it was also the very same bed in which Grandmother had breathed her last, a bed for life and death, in short; a bed for love, too, now that the lovers have come from behind the tightly-stretched gauze and are lying down on it. The musicians start their pantomime. Ramming the violin so hard into my chest that I can hardly breathe, I start improvising, making sure I follow the aleatory bowing of the instrumentalist. Occasionally the half-naked dancers, garlanded with flowers, waving their arms around, get between the camera and the bed. Which is irritating. You would also prefer the camera to come closer, so you can get a bit more from some of the details, but you can quite clearly see that Gyf has kept his glasses on, a sunbeam is reflected in their lenses. The young woman is on top of him now, her legs tucked round her lover's recumbent body, and she's starting to make a slight swaying movement with her bust, as if she was sitting on one of those little mobile seats they have in boats in rowing competitions. Her mass of hair has fallen over her face so it's not possible to appreciate the beauty of her features, but we can trust Gyf. Her breasts too remain veiled, it's infuriating, when all she need have done was toss her head back, but you only have to ask, because at the same time she pushes a strand of hair out of her eyes, although this doesn't help you to see much of her bosom, yet a nasty feeling suddenly comes over you, a kind of suspicion, you seem to recognise that gesture, and it doesn't take long to go through the list of candidates: Tell me, Theo, it surely wasn't you? You would like to get it clear in your mind, which is why, Gyf, I don't want to dictate to you, you're the director, but how about a close-up now, or a zoom in, instead of that long static shot, wouldn't that give you a chance, once the camera's rolling, to close in on the objective, and what an objective, isn't it, but don't you think a genuine revolutionary like you ought to give a bit of thought to other people now and then, all the more so in that, without wanting to criticise, you did keep the best part for yourself, it didn't occur to you to get a stand-in to fondle the beauty's breasts greedily the way you're doing now, charity begins at home, yet would it be too much to ask if one were to beg a few crumbs from this love feast, no strings attached, just the right to look, something in the spirit of that poor devil a hotelkeeper dragged to court and accused of sniffing at the odours coming from his kitchen through a venti-lator, but, luckily for him, for the poor beggar who got his nourishment from the vapours of a great delicacy, in those days you did sometimes come across a judge who was a righteous man, so much so in this case that they canonised him in the hope that his fellow judges would take a leaf out of his book, because this was Saint Yves, and do you know what he did after he had heard the plaintiff? He tossed up the coin the hotelkeeper had demanded as compensation and, when it bounced on the floor, pronounced his sentence: The sound pays for the smell. That was how he did justice in Brittany in the old days, one of your two patron saints, and don't forget the other one, Saint George. So kindly slay the dragon of doubt, do us the justice of agreeing that we have a right to the truth, show us the naked truth. So: Theo or not Theo? Her secret or not her secret?

NOR DID I EVER find out what Gyf had written on the slate. Perhaps a tribute to beauty, or a poem, or a question about art, or a definitive statement on the meaning of existence. Perhaps quite simply the name of the heroine. At all events, in response to his nod I had acquiesced, no point in going back on it. And that was just as well, because it looked as if it would be difficult to go back on it now. At the moment when a fleeting image on the taut sheet showed the lover's profile, her head thrown back and offered up to the sun, at the moment when it finally seemed possible that light was about to be shed on the whole thing, I poked my bow between the spokes of the reel, the way you put a finger to your lips to call for silence, and it stopped running as if by magic. Because the exasperating thing about films is that they are always in movement, incapable of taking a stand against the march of time, against the inexorable agony of things, incapable of suggesting an alternative to that shot-by-shot entropy of living forces – and if the beauty was Theo, it was worth pausing, taking one's time, it was worth a glance. All I had to do was stretch out an arm, avoid her shadow on the screen, and go up a bit closer: If this really is your secret, Theo, it's not going to remain secret for much longer.

Not for much longer, indeed: a dark spot appeared in the centre of the image, and in no time spread like a drop of ink on a piece of blotting paper, gangrening the film, caramelising the nudity of the two bodies, then the profile of the girl, and her hair, soon swamping the entire image, burrowing into it, restoring the whiteness of the screen, while a thin wisp of smoke rose up over the projector. I whisked the bow out, but it was already too late to solve the mystery of the heroine. A thimble would have sufficed to hold the feather-light ashes fluttering round in the cowshed. The guitarist, his eyes closed, beating time on the mud floor with his foot, his face shrouded in the smoke of the cigarette burning down in his fingers, was too far away to notice any damage caused by my pause on the image. Taking advantage of my defection, he was once again giving voice, once again calling on his Mama, immured in his alimentary demands, impervious to the heady question of love being posed a stone's throw away on a taut sheet flooded with light. It was time to make myself scarce.

I left the magic glasses in a prominent position on the kitchen table. They hadn't taught me anything I didn't already suspect. That's to say: the same frames that made me blanch with terror and wish the earth would swallow me up when I wore them – these very same glasses, on Gyf's button nose, didn't scare the girls off at the crucial moment. Apart from that, specs or no specs you couldn't see any better. There was a pencil on the table by the cat's dish, and I hastily scribbled across a sheet of paper, in large letters: Gyf, your film is magnificent – and I wasn't just being polite, because I only had to ask myself honestly what film had ever made such a profound impression on me? And however hard I thought back and turned over in my mind all my greatest cinematic memories – and I used to go to the movies every week at the time – this *Tomb* was more beautiful, more intense, truer, more moving, more dramatic, more intriguing, and also funnier (from the point of view of destiny, be it understood) than any film I had yet seen. More ephemeral, too. This was no time to hang about. Hearing that on the floor above the reunion of Equivocality and Paradox was making a bit of a noise, I had put my violin back in its case and was cautiously closing the two halves of the door at the very moment when I heard Gyf's voice wondering where on earth the funny smell in his loft could be coming from.

Not wanting the sound of the engine to attract anyone's attention, I pushed my Solex up to the end of the path, repressing, metre by metre, the temptation to turn back, although the farther I went the more unlikely this became. My conscience was not entirely clear, but after all Gyf had certainly asked for it. He had been dreaming of a film-non-film. Well, he had one, and one that was even more radical: a film-no-film-at-all. This auto-da-fé was the apotheosis of his aesthetic conceptions, a perfectly revolutionary act, probably the first and last example of a Mongo-Aoustinian art.

It was dark, now, and the moon, ambushed behind dense clouds, was diffusing an inky light over the surrounding countryside, so I had to start the engine if I wanted to light my way. This involved the classic manoeuvre by which you recognise the professionals. You run along beside the putt-putting machine, and once the engine gets going you jump up on to the triangular saddle. Up till now this acrobatic routine had presented no problem. But on this occasion, whether on account of my precipitous departure, my moonlight flit, my fear of hearing a voice demanding an explanation of this new version of Joan of Arc, or Yvette, or Theo (now both also at the stake), the fact remains that the front wheel suddenly jack-knifed, bringing the Solex to an abrupt halt and projecting me over the handlebars with some violence. I waited until I had resumed contact with the earth for my brain to take advantage of this loop the loop and flash me the speeded-up film of my life, a florilegium of its key moments. In this way I was hoping to find out which sequences had most marked me, and not necessarily the ones I would myself have chosen: death, bereavements, Fraslin, the beautiful drowned girl, and similar vexations, and to discover whatever detail it was that had escaped me even though it had influenced the future course of my existence, like the stone that diverts a stream at its source and which is ultimately responsible for the Loire flowing into the Atlantic and not into the Mediterranean. But perhaps there hadn't been anything particularly striking that I didn't already know, or nothing worth bothering about, or any wish to relive anything I had already lived through, or perhaps my brain had seized up. Hence this night flight, this touch of amnesia before again hitting the ground, or rather the water, because the ditch on the receiving end of my fall hadn't yet been drained of the last few days' rain, and never would be, no doubt, except maybe during the years of drought, and it was just as well we didn't happen to be in the months of such years because my return to earth was thereby cushioned, and even quite pleasant.

Curiously enough, my first thought was not to rejoice at still being on this side of the world and apparently undamaged, but for the paternal harvest promised for survivors, thus reviving an old memory when, playing my very first football match, I was biting the dusty grass after someone had intercepted me in one of my glorious dribbles. The prediction came back to me: As he sowed, so shall you reap. But the only harvest I could see was the badly-maintained grass on the pitch, the animosity of the other players, and my solitude. And if, despite my teammates' injunctions, I had taken my time in getting up again, it was because I didn't want to let them enjoy the sight of my tears, which is always a triumph for some, when I knew that all the fathers were on the touchline protecting their progeniture, except for the one who had gone for good, because if he had been there, the commander, my very present help in time of trouble, the brute who knocked me over would never have dared.

This time too, with my nose in my refrigerated paddy field, the crop was meagre and boded no good for the future. Yet there was one thing: I couldn't see how I could ever fall any lower, for anything lower would at the very least mean that I was dead. So I had proof that I had now touched bottom, and after that moment destiny's mocking little smile, with which I was so familiar, was transformed into something that could almost have been joy. A limited joy, no doubt, but, just like that dark spot in the centre of the screen a little while ago, sure of itself, quite prepared to take everything over, a joy like a fire raiser, so, having extracted myself from my swamp without too many bruises but wet through and frozen stiff, I straightened the handlebars, harnessed the violin case once again on the luggage rack, wedged my sports bag down over the crank gear, pushed the engine lever forward, ran, my feet sloshing in my shoes, along the side of the Solex, and, when I was just about to jump on to the saddle, weighed down by my reefer jacket which I thought I might now call my mess jacket, I imagined that it was the seabed I was kicking off from, which is what divers say they do when they want to come back up to the surface, fancying that something had just turned upside down, or perhaps the Earth had tipped over, but that this movement was certainly going to help me, because once I was back on the surface, who could prevent someone who had escaped the waters from continuing on his momentum, making himself weightless, lighter than air, rising ever higher, reaching the troposphere, the stratosphere, the exosphere? And then, while the chubby little headlight wedged between the two cylindrical cheeks of the tank and the sump was piercing the Earth's night, I was already smiling at the thought of the moment when, at the very pinnacle of my triumphal assumption, the new star of the awestruck heavens would throw herself into my outstretched arms.

JEAN ROUAUD, who won the Prix Goncourt, France's most prestigious literary prize, with his first novel, *Fields of Glory,* at the age of thirty-eight – not for forty years had it gone to a hitherto unpublished author – earned his living as a nightwatchman, a stagehand, a philosophy teacher and a newsvendor in Paris before the success of that novel enabled him to turn to fulltime writing. He has since published two further highly acclaimed novels by way of sequel, *Of Illustrious Men,* and this present one.

BARBARA WRIGHT is translator of Jean Rouaud's previous novel, *Of Illustrious Men,* with which she won the first Weidenfeld Translation Prize. She is three times winner of the Scott Moncrieff Prize. Authors she has translated include Raymond Queneau, Nathalie Sarraute and Robert Pinget.